TUCKAHOE
SLIDEBOTTLE

TUCKAHOE
SLIDEBOTTLE

❧ ❧

NEIL
MCKINNON

thistledown press

Library and Archives Canada Cataloguing in Publication

McKinnon, Neil, 1941-
Tuckahoe slidebottle / Neil McKinnon.

ISBN 1-897235-07-0

I. Title.

PS8625.K556T82 2006   C813'.6   C2006-903734-5

Cover photograph ©Trinette Reed/zefa/Corbis
Cover and book design by Jackie Forrie
Typeset by Thistledown Press
Printed and bound in Canada

Thistledown Press Ltd.
633 Main Street
Saskatoon, Saskatchewan, S7H 0J8
www.thistledownpress.com

Thistledown Press gratefully acknowledges the financial assistance of the Canada Council for the Arts, the Saskatchewan Arts Board, and the Government of Canada through the Book Publishing Industry Development Program for its publishing program.

ACKNOWLEDGEMENTS

A book does not happen overnight. A publisher once told me that the average time from when a neophyte puts pen to paper until the work appears in a bookstore is about ten years. Fortunately he told me that long after I'd first put pen to paper. It has been an extended journey but I've had help along the way and no writer ever had a better team of encouragers. Special thanks are owed to the following: Graham Chandler and Patrick Carmichael, the Tuesday Night Nitters who patiently listened to every word of every story and then made invaluable suggestions; Gloria Sawai and the Banff Centre Writing Program for teaching me how to be critical of my own work; Alejandro Grattan and the Ajijic Writer's Group for providing a venue to test the stories, for offering valuable criticism and for being great friends; Larry Reeves and the former Ajijic Storytellers for giving me a public reading forum; Diane Tucker, my editor, for her critical eye. I owe more than I can ever repay to members of my family: my mother, Selma Coyle, for starting it all; my daughters, Kristy and Kelty McKinnon, and son-in-law Richard LeHingrat for reading and commenting on some of the stories; my wife, Judy, who is my best friend and my best critic, and who has been with me every step of the way.

The poetry quoted in "Love, Poetry and Seagulls" was excerpted from: "She Walks in Beauty" by Lord Byron; "Annabel Lee" by Edgar Allen Poe; "It Is Not Always May" and "The Rainy Day" by Henry Wadsworth Longfellow; "She Dwelt Among the Untrodden Ways" by William Wordsworth; "Delight in Disorder" by Robert Herrick; "Song" by Aphra Behn; "Pied Beauty" by Gerard Manley Hopkins; "To Helen" by Edgar Allen Poe; "Meeting at Night" by Robert Browning; "How Do I Love Thee? (*Sonnets from the Portuguese* XLIII)" by Elizabeth Barrett Browning; "To one that asked me why I lov'd J.G." by Ephelia; "To Virgins, to Make Much of Time" by Robert Herrick; "Wild nights-wild nights! (*Love* XXV)" by Emily Dickinson;

CONTENTS

For Callum

U-Turns Under *the* Sheets

The town itself is homeless. It lies on the prairie like a drunk on a sidewalk. In winter, snow packs down and turns to ice. Kids hold on to bumpers and slide on floppy overshoes. The cold makes smoke fall from chimneys. It crawls along frozen streets until the town is hazy and smells of burning wood. People scurry to the small buildings in their backyards, disappear inside and rush, shivering, back to the warmth of kitchen stoves. It's not a time to be outside and without the smoke you might think no one lived here.

In summer, Russian thistle and stinging nettle grow beside neglected buildings huddled along rutted streets. Dried potholes slam your teeth as you drive. Dust rolls past when you stop. The dirt road into town ends at Louie's Café — once a gambling hall, open day and night. Now Louie puts a *Closed For Lunch* sign in the window. There is nothing to do and those who do it well congregate in front of Louie's.

The town is called Tuckahoe. The usual folks had gathered to do nothing the day my cousin Isaac walked in from the highway. A dozen eyes watched him strut down Main Street. Dust squirted from his heels at each step. He had his gut sucked in, his chest stuck out and his butt shoved way behind him. His head moved back and forth like it wasn't sure if it should be above his chest or his rear-end.

"He looks like a horny little dog trying to hump a rolling soccer ball," Blind Clarence Archer observed. Blind Clarence acquired his name because of an inability to see any point of view other than his own. His eyesight was fine.

Isaac dumped his duffel bag in the dirt in front of Louie's. Cool as willow shade and with sweat dripping from his chin he grinned at The Jury.

The Jury was five or six tobacco chewers and sunflower-seed-spitters who met every day to pass judgement on the private lives of others. They spent summers wagging chins in front of Louie's. Winters were spent wagging chins in the Cenotaph Hotel Beer Parlour.

Isaac pulled a half-smoked butt from his shirt pocket and lit up. "Where can a man get a cold beer?" he asked. "And anyone tell me where I can find Daryl Robertson?"

His mouth barely moved when he talked, so words fought their way out between his front teeth. He was dressed like a cowboy on top and at the bottom. Between his Stetson and high-heeled boots, he wore parts of an old army uniform.

Baldy Potter uncurled himself from the bench in front of the café and stepped from under the awning into the afternoon glare. "Depends who wants to know, and why you want to know," he said. A roll-your-own bobbed in the southeast corner of his unshaven face.

"My name's Isaac Talbot. I'm a nephew to Daryl Robertson's missus. Do you know where I can find him?" He pushed back his Stetson and swiped at the sweat on his forehead.

Old Alex Kinnear was resting his chin on his chest, contemplating his boots. He lifted his red whiskey face, peered from one eye over a bush of whiskers, sucked in his cheeks and spat a stream of tobacco juice. It landed between Isaac's boots. "Isaac Talbot, eh?" he squeaked. "Your initials spell 'IT'. Gawddam fella, you look like an IT."

Sunlight reflected from sweat glistening on Baldy's unprotected dome. He scuttled back under the awning. "This is your lucky day, IT. Your beer and Daryl are at the same place — in the pub around the corner."

Isaac picked up his bag. "Thanks for nothing," he said.

Baldy grinned at Isaac's back as he walked away. He ran his hand over his head and pushed moisture down the back of his neck. Ashes fell from his roll-your-own as he rendered judgement. "He don't look like he has an enemy in the world, but I betcha most of his friends don't like him much."

"Maybe not," Alex shrilled. "But I bet he's got a heart so big he wouldn't spend all his girlfriend's money on soap."

Blind Clarence roused himself from his perch on Louie's window ledge. Clearly the situation begged for learned commentary. "A wise man said we're all a dream in the mind of God, but he looks more like a nightmare in the brain of an idiot," he pronounced.

The case was closed. In The Jury's verdicts, candour defeated kindness every time.

≈ ≈

A stranger in Tuckahoe was news. Isaac's arrival immediately replaced the weather as the main topic of conversation. I heard about him before he got to the beer parlour.

I was fourteen that summer. My name is Alan but everyone called me Obbie. Mom said it was short for Obstacle because I was always underfoot when I was small. My dad, Daryl Robertson, disagreed. He said Obbie was short for Obstinate.

Isaac was Mom's nephew, just out of the army. He was a skinny stretch with a small pot where he stored beer on Saturday nights. He wasn't thirty, but his sandy hair was already thin on top. He told me it got that way from doing U-turns under the sheets, but his sex life had become like his hairline — mainly receded.

Dad brought him out to the farm and he stayed to work. I liked him right off. He sometimes called me kid, but he was the first grown-up to treat me as an equal. I now realise that said more about his level of maturity than mine.

Trouble followed Isaac in from the highway. He was single, he was breathing and, when he wasn't drinking, he was vertical. This made him desirable to ladies who had missed the draw in the local marriage bonspiel.

I said trouble followed him, but that's wrong. It went ahead and waited for him around every corner. He usually caught up quick. Responsibility and Isaac weren't on speaking terms, so he was easily detoured by enticing mixtures of back seats, lonely girls, and whiskey — situations that sometimes compelled him to say things he didn't mean. By winter, it was rumoured he had three women leaving doors unlocked as they waited for a promised ring. None of them pushed hard. None, that is, until he tangled with Vicki Barstow.

As usual, when he was drunk, Isaac up and proposed, but Vicki didn't co-operate like the others. She outweighed Isaac by forty pounds and she didn't like waiting. He told me she tried all the tricks: crying, yelling, threats, silence and sex. He said sex and threats were the most persuasive but he told her marriage wasn't going to happen. She went straight to her dad. Vicki's old man was big and real mean, and nobody crossed him. He threatened to beat the crap out of Isaac and made him buy an engagement ring.

The Jury spent an afternoon sequestered in the beer parlour deliberating about Isaac's problem. Baldy shook his head and gazed at the glass of draft in front of him. "IT sees responsibility different than other folks, kind of like a load he's carrying in a bucket. When it gets heavy, he just dumps some out," he said.

"Not always," Alex replied. "Sometimes he hands it to one of his friends, and sometimes he slops the whole thing on fate or bad luck."

Anyway, Vicki was showing her shiny new ring all over town, telling everybody she was going home with Isaac at Christmas to meet his folks.

☙ ❧

One Saturday, Mom sent me to call him for lunch. It was one of those winter days when the sun is brilliant but still loses hands down to the temperature. All it can do is glisten up ice crystals as they slide in frozen air. Snow squeaked under my overshoes. My breath grabbed my face and turned white as I walked down to the corral.

Isaac was doctoring a bloated steer and I climbed to the top rail to watch. The animal, belly bulged out, was snubbed to a pole. He had just stabbed the steer and he held the scissors with both hands to keep the wound open. It bellered and bucked, but I could see gas escaping in the cold air.

Isaac screwed up his face. "GeeVee KeeReist, Obbie, this stinks wors'en an army john the morning after payday."

I jumped down and took over holding the scissors. As the pressure eased, the animal quieted. "Thanks," he said. "I thought I was going to die from the smell."

He stepped back and watched the steamy gas escaping from the hole in the steer's belly. "Say, Obbie, I got a favour to ask. It's important. You got to promise not to tell nobody. If you do it — who knows? You know I'm going home for Christmas. Maybe your folks will let you come along."

My heart did a flip-flop. "Do you think they'll let me? Are we gonna take the train? Do we stop in Saskatoon? How long will we be gone?" I forgot to move my feet and got stepped on. The steer was feeling a lot better.

"GeeVee, don't go getting your hopes too high, kid. Your folks still gotta say okay. Yeah, we'll take the train and yeah, we'll stop in Saskatoon."

My brain worked faster than a weasel in a henhouse. I really wanted to go. In my entire fourteen years I'd never been farther than fifty miles from Tuckahoe. And spending time in Saskatoon . . . geez, I'd never been in a town bigger than Stoneboat Creek.

"Sure, Isaac! What do you want me to do?"

"I need some things from town and nobody should know. I want a box of Dodd's Kidney Pills, and get me a sunlamp at Freed's Store. It's this cold weather. I think my kidneys are ailing, and maybe the sunlamp will do something for the cracks in my hands."

🖙 🖘

I was so excited I didn't even wonder why he was inviting me, but I found out a couple of days later. Vicki cornered me in the back booth in Louie's. "I hear you're going with Isaac to his folks' place for Christmas," she said.

I wasn't sure how to answer. She was as big and tough as any guy, and her eyes looked like my dog's before he shakes the bejeesus out of a garter snake. All of a sudden I understood. Isaac wanted me to go *because* of Vicki. He needed an excuse not to take her.

Before I could think of an answer she grabbed my ears and stuck her face in mine. She was chewing gum but I could still tell she'd had kolbassa for lunch. "If Isaac takes you instead of me, I'll remove your personal equipment with rusty barbed wire," she sneered. She got up and tramped out.

Vicki had made my scalp tighten up and I thought about not going. I found Isaac splashing gas into the trough heater and told him what she'd said. He gazed at the clouds and hooked his thumbs inside the army web belt he claimed was handy in fights. The Jury had doubts about his fights. Clarence said they ranked up there with other fine fiction, like *Tobacco Road* or Isaac's description of his own sex life.

"Did she scare you, kid?" Isaac asked.

"Yeah, she makes me nervous. How come she doesn't scare you?"

He scratched a match and dropped it in the fire box. It exploded into flames and we both jumped. He laughed and rubbed singed eyebrows. "Oh, she does, kid, she does. I just got more practice hiding it. Welcome to the club. That's what makes the world go round — raw, naked fear. Everybody's afraid of something: fear of war, fear of growing old, fear of not getting married, and my favourite, fear of getting married. Sheer terror: it's the best motivation there is. Probably gets more folks off their ass than money does."

He clammed up and poked around in the roaring fire box. I figured he'd decided to let Vicki take a round out of me and to take his chances with her old man. I didn't say anything but I didn't think him being afraid of marriage was a good reason for me to get beat up.

🙢 🙢

About a week later I was in town with Isaac when we met Vicki and her father on Main Street. Mr. Barstow laid right into him. "Talbot, I been looking all over for you."

We both backed up a few steps. He was loud and he didn't look friendly.

"Yes, sir! I been around. I ain't been hiding."

"Talbot, we been looking for you 'cause Vicki's changed her mind. She don't want no part of you. She wouldn't marry you if you were the last man in the country . . . and I sure as hell don't want you for no son-in-law." Mr. Barstow never did have trouble saying exactly what was on his mind.

"What do you mean, Barstow? You don't want me in your family?" He shuffled his cowboy boots in the snow. "Shucks, I been looking forward to calling you Daddy." He looked at Vicki. "You're not backing out on me now, are you, Sugar Pie?" He lit a roll-your-own and blew smoke rings at the sky. He didn't sound disappointed — more like he'd got the blackout at a car bingo.

Vicki started to cry, only no tears came; just her nose started up. She made a noise like a wounded chicken, took the ring off her finger and tossed it at Isaac. Then she and her old man turned and high-tailed it down the street. I didn't understand and Isaac was no help. He just grinned and blew more smoke rings.

I got the whole story anyway. Everything that happened in Tuckahoe was passed around fast. Keeping something private was like using your hands to scoop water into a hot radiator: no matter how careful you are, some trickles out. The town had it figured out quicker than a horse kick. The break-up was the main jaw exerciser in the beer parlour for the rest of the winter.

☙ ❧

The Cenotaph Hotel Beer Parlour was cool and dark and smelled like stale beer and tobacco. Norman Rockwell *Saturday Evening Post* covers hung on plywood walls. The bar stretched along the back. A dozen round tables were scattered in front, easy spitting distance from brass spittoons. The terrycloth-covered tables were usually occupied by members of The Jury.

Dirty Bernie's table stood alone on the far side of the room, grease marks on the wall behind it. Bernie had once been a problem for Hank, the owner of the hotel. He hadn't washed or changed clothes since anyone could remember, although he had scrubbed a small area on his chest when the TB van came to town and he had to have an X-ray. He passed his non-drinking hours working in the grease pit at Mac's Garage. Over time, a lot of grease had been transferred from the garage to the Cenotaph. Most of his salary was spent in the beer parlour and Hank didn't want to lose the business, so Bernie was required to sit at the same table every day. Hank kept it reserved for him.

On the Saturday before the breakup with Vicki, Isaac sat with Bernie, Old Alex, and Baldy, all three of whom were capable of spreading news faster than the radio. When Isaac offered to buy, they welcomed him as one of their own.

"Gentlemen," Isaac said, as Hank delivered the first round, "a toast." He raised his glass. "To good times and good health." He clinked each glass and drained his own. The others solemnly followed suit.

Old Alex put his glass down. "Gawddam, IT. I don't know much about good health, but I know somethin' about good times. These old coots been chasin' good times so hard they got blinded by their own sweat and ran right past. The good times are all behind them now."

Isaac grinned and lit a tailor-made. He signalled for a second round, and followed it with another. Soon they found their rhythm. Beer flowed. Ashtrays were filled and emptied. Voices rose and fell. Camaraderie converged on the small fraternity like sparrows on warm horse manure.

Bernie was the first to take a break. "I gotta go to the little boy's room," he said. "Gotta make sure the old tap still runs." He walked unsteadily toward the toilet at the back of the bar.

Isaac stood up. "Me, too," he said. "Hank, bring another round while I'm gone." His face looked like a boy's when he's lying in the grass waiting for a gopher to stick its head up inside a snare loop.

A few seconds later the two stood side by side at the tin trough that drained away most of the beer sold in the Cenotaph. While two streams drummed on the tin, each man focused on the wall facing him, observing the unwritten code that allows a measure of privacy in the most crowded of beer-passing circumstances. The code dictates that, apart from a quick glance down during the ritual shake at the end, no one is to let his eye stray lest embarrassment ensue, or worse still, someone get the wrong idea.

Isaac let out a low whistle. "GeeVee Kee*reist*! Will you look at that! It's turned green!"

Dirty Bernie involuntarily let his gaze drop, just far enough to see a bright green stream cascading from Isaac into the trough. "Gawddam, IT! Something in you ain't working right. What the hell's wrong?" Bernie eased away. "Have you got something that's catching?" he asked in a hushed voice.

"Damn! Damn!" Isaac looked down at the green flow. "I seen this once before in the army. It's the *dreaded lurgy*. First there's this green stuff, and then . . . KeeReist, it develops into the *creeping scringe*."

"The creeping scringe!" Bernie moved down to the far end of the trough. "What the hell are you talking about? You got *two* things wrong with you?"

Isaac finished and tucked himself away. "Yeah, I probably do. The scringe follows the lurgy. You know you've got it when your skin peels off. It starts on your chest and spreads." He turned toward Bernie, unbuttoning his shirt. "KeeReist, Bernie, get a load of this!"

Bernie backed up against the wall. "Gawddam, IT. Stay away from me! Your whole chest's peelin' off! There's skin everywhere! Where did you get it? Is it catching? Are you gonna die?"

Isaac rebuttoned his shirt. "Damn right it's catching. I probably got it in one of them ill-repute houses overseas. That's why they call them that. They got a reputation for making you sick. But this is only symptoms. The next stage is worse. That's when things really fall apart."

"What do you mean, fall apart? What's the next stage? No! Don't you come near me!" Bernie had his hand on the doorknob, ready to bolt.

"GeeVee, Bernie, you should feel sorry for me. What I got is European leprosy. Like I said, I seen it before. It don't look good for me. First the skin comes off, like you seen. Then the fingers and toes go. Next, I'll lose my ears and nose . . . and eventually even my privates fall off. But I don't think you'll get it unless you breathed in fumes while I was whizzin'. Besides, I doubt those leprosy germs could get through all that grease to get inside you, anyway. But whatever you do, Bernie, don't tell those other guys. I don't want to scare them and I don't want it spread all over town, now that I'm getting married. Promise me you won't say nothing, okay?"

"Yeah . . . yeah, sure . . . whatever." Bernie opened the door and scurried out.

Isaac waited a few minutes. By the time he stepped out, the regulars had all left. Hank had a puzzled look on his face. The chairs were empty. Full glasses had been abandoned. Isaac walked over, sat down, scratched his chest, and resumed drinking.

🦅 🦅

On the train heading out of Tuckahoe, Isaac leaned back in the seat and grinned. "GeeVee, I hope you appreciate all I done for you, Obbie. I damn near put myself in the hospital just to keep Vicki from making you a permanent member of the ladies' choir."

"What do you mean, put yourself in the hospital? You're healthy as a horse."

"Not really," he said. "First, I nearly fried my chest laying under that GeeVee sunlamp for almost five hours; then I took so damn many kidney pills I pissed green for three days. You owe me a big thank you, kid."

"Yeah, I guess I do. Thanks a lot. But it seems to me you done yourself a huge favour, too."

He nodded, leaned back and closed his eyes. I could see our reflections in the train window and, through them, miles of moonlight on white snow. Flickering yardlights lit up distant farmhouses as we clacked our way between tiny prairie towns.

OLD ALEX *and the* FIRE

Tuckahoe looked the same — a tiny forgotten island in a prairie sea. Dusty poplars, limp in the heat, framed unpainted houses. Gophers frolicked on vacant lots: popping up, running, flicking tails and disappearing faster than my eye could follow. *There's more of them here than people*, I thought. *And tomorrow, when we bury Old Alex, there'll be one less person.*

A broken hitching post still marked the entrance to the Cenotaph Hotel Beer Parlour. Across the street, railway tracks kept five weathered grain elevators in line, faded orange and red sentinels buffering town from encroaching prairie. Two boys, playing by the tracks, threw firecrackers in the air, then laughed and dodged as they popped and fell to the ground.

There were no customers in the beer parlour. I ordered a cold one to wash away the dust. Nothing had changed. Even the grease marks by Dirty Bernie's table were still on the wall. Twenty-five years slipped away. I could almost hear Alex's high-pitched nasal voice saying, "I know who lit that fire!"

🦢 🦢

Old Alex ran the livery stable, when he wasn't in the beer parlour complaining that nobody used horses anymore. He hid his face behind a mass of grey and white whiskers which he carried about four feet above his boots. On Saturdays he used a silver dollar to cover the hole where his left eye was supposed to be. Usually he wore a black eye patch, but Saturday night was Saturday night, and Alex was from the old school. He believed in dressing up for his weekly night of drinking and socialising. The fact that he drank and socialised on the other six days as well didn't deter him.

Saturday was when most farm women came to town and Alex fancied himself a sport. Women, however, were not allowed in the beer parlour, so few had actually seen Alex at his best: rosy face shining, large smile full of tobacco-teeth and his beard stained yellow, burnt in the corner where the roll-your-own dangled. All this was set off by the shining silver dollar.

When we were growing up we all loved Old Alex. He told us his eye was shot out in the Great War and one of the Kaiser's bullets was lodged in his brain. "That's why I got to run this here livery stable, kids. I can't see to shoot no more, so I lost my job as Tom Mix's sidekick."

On Saturday nights, after the beer parlour closed, he'd weave the two blocks to his shack behind the livery barn. Sometimes he sang *Mother Machree* in a loud voice. If we asked him, he'd take the silver dollar out of his eye and flip us, heads or tails, for our weekly allowances. We paid little attention to the bet, as we were trying to look into Old Alex's head, each hoping to spot the German bullet. Of course we never did, and he usually won our money. We didn't mind. It was a fair trade, and besides, he always spent his winnings on firecrackers which he helped us set off over by the railway tracks.

≈≋ ≋

My name is Alan Robertson, although folks in Tuckahoe still call me Obbie. I was twenty-one and home from university when the Pool elevator burned to the ground. Fighting the fire was useless. Flames overwhelmed the night. We watched until the rising sun left only wisps of smoke visible in the sky. That evening my father said arson was suspected and the Mounties were looking into it. He also said insurance investigators would be nosing around.

A few days later two strangers driving a blue '59 Buick ahead of a cloud of dust, pulled up in front of Louie's. The dust settled on The Jury, sequestered under the awning in front of the café.

"They ain't from around here. Geez," Baldy Potter whispered in awe, "they might even be Easterners."

The driver stepped out, tapping his nose with a handkerchief. He was wearing a light blue suit and a confused predatory look, like a fox in a henhouse trying to decide which chicken to eat. His black hair was slick and shiny. "I'm Richard Blanchard," he said. "This is my partner, Charles Penhallurick. We're here to investigate the fire and we need a place to stay. Is there anything decent in this dump?"

He turned up his nose and then looked down it. "We won't be here any longer than we have to. I can promise you that."

Penhallurick stood behind Blanchard. His eyes shifted back and forth as if we were all guilty of a serious offence and he was trying to decide who to execute.

Baldy straightened his slouch. "Well Dick and Chuck, it depends on what you're lookin' for. The Cenotaph Hotel is around the corner and they wash the sheets after every third customer. They put clean water in the bathtub every Saturday. It's only Tuesday so you won't need a shovel to get into it. I don't think they've had more than three or four people stay since the weekend."

Blind Clarence Archer stared at Blanchard. "Nobody's been bitten by a bedbug in almost a week. They killed most of 'em when they sprayed for the cockroaches," he said.

Dirty Bernie picked grease from his eyebrows and rubbed it on his trousers. Then he picked grease from his trousers and rubbed it in his eyebrows. "That's true," he mused. "But I think it helped when Hank started dumping the chamber pots instead of letting them sit 'til they was full."

As the oldest member of The Jury, Blind Clarence was used to having the last word. "There ain't been so many rats in the hotel since Hank caught that big rattler in the coulees and turned it loose," he announced solemnly. "You boys'll be in luxury over there."

The investigators turned and headed for the Cenotaph, hurrying as if fleeing a bad smell. They entered the beer parlour and sat down at Dirty Bernie's table.

"Sorry gentlemen, you have to move," Hank Klassen told them, coming around the bar and motioning to another table. "This one's reserved." The back of Blanchard's suit displayed a pattern of black grease.

Blanchard and Penhallurick stayed at the hotel. They slept late, and after trying Hank's cooking once, they usually walked down to Louie's for breakfast. They tried jawing with the morning crew in front of the café, but they didn't fit in. Nick Fedorich spent most of his waking and some of his sleeping hours holding up the outside wall of the café. "They talk like they got two by fours shoved up their rears keepin' their backs straight and their noses in the air," he said.

Later, they'd wander down to the Cenotaph and spend the rest of the day sipping small glasses of draft. They let it be known they'd buy for anyone who would talk to them about the fire. A few of the regulars tried, but lost interest when they found the investigators wanted real information. Consequently, Blanchard's and Penhallurick's generosity went untapped.

Untapped, that is, until one hot afternoon when we all heard Old Alex loudly proclaim, "I know who lit that fire!" The room came to attention and conversation skidded to a stop. Blind Clarence leaned forward. He had trouble hearing.

Baldy Potter grinned. "What do you mean, you know who lit that fire, you old goat? Hell, you don't know nothin'. In fact, you know less than that. You wouldn't know a good time if it walked over and sat on your lap."

"You got it, Baldy." Bernie had entered unnoticed and settled in his reserved chair.

Alex bristled. "Don't tell me what I know or don't know, you hairless dick. I know what I know, and I know who lit that fire . . . and I don't need no penis with ears telling me what a good time is neether."

Baldy ignored Alex. "What you doin' here, Bernie?" he asked. "I hope you changed the oil in my car."

"Changed your oil! I guess not! That wreck of yours would up and die if it smelt new oil. You ain't never changed the oil in that car. I did the same as I always do, topped it up with used tractor oil." Bernie grinned and scratched the grease in his eyebrows.

"Here you are, fellas. Compliments of the two gents over there." Hank arrived with a round, bottles rather than the draft they'd been drinking.

Everyone nodded to Blanchard and Penhallurick, and then each intently studied the label on his bottle. Soon two chairs slid up to the terrycloth-covered table. "Mind if we join you gentlemen?" Blanchard asked.

"Not at all, fellas," Alex said. He looked like a boy who'd just convinced his mother he was too sick to go to school on Game Seven day of the World Series.

Bernie continued. "You know Baldy, one of these days I'm going to have to charge you for the tractor oil. The way your car goes through it, Mac's going to notice some missing."

"Charge me, you tightwad. You just throw that stuff out. It ain't good for nothin' except keepin' down road dust."

Blanchard made a face and edged away from Bernie. Impatient, he signalled Hank for another round. "Did somebody say he knows who lit the elevator fire?" he asked, and looked at each face around the table.

"That'd be Alex," Baldy volunteered. "But don't pay no attention. He's always either drunk or dreamin' or hallucinatin'. Sometimes he does all three at once. In any case, he just plain don't know what's happenin' around him."

"You got a point, Baldy," Bernie said. "But sometimes he gets things right. Remember his towing company? I hear he made a fortune on that venture."

Alex got up and headed for the toilet. Everyone grinned. They all knew the story of how, during spring runoff, a low-lying piece of road on the edge of town had become impassable. How Alex had used a team of horses he was boarding at the livery barn to pull vehicles through the muck. How he had charged the limit and been rolling in profits until someone saw him, at midnight, hauling water out to the road to prolong the muddy conditions. The story got out and most of Alex's previous customers came and collected their money back. To add financial ruin to insult, the horses' owner demanded compensation for the use of his team. It was the only time in living memory that Alex had made himself scarce around the beer parlour. No one was sure whether he was broke or embarrassed, but he stayed away for almost three days. When he finally showed up, he sat by himself for another two days, a period of self-imposed silence that became legendary when someone pointed out that, for the entire time, he'd bought his own beer.

By the time Alex returned from the toilet, Baldy was bending Penhallurick's ear with *his* theory of how the fire started. There was another round on the table.

"It wasn't arson," Baldy said. "It was spontaneous combustion. Kids was smokin' over there by the annex and one of them threw his butt away. It started from that . . . spontaneously."

Blanchard sighed into the laughter. "Afraid not. We're sure it was deliberate. Hey Hank, keep the beer coming over here. Who do you think lit the fire, Alex?"

"WHAT DO YOU MEAN, THINK? I KNOW WHO LIT THAT FIRE," Alex yelled. He pounded on the table and the bottles jumped. Blind Clarence grinned.

"No offence," Blanchard hastened to assure him. "Here, let me buy another round." By this time the beer was stacked up in front of Alex. He spent the next few minutes reducing the line-up. Everyone watched as he drained the last bottle. Blanchard nodded to Hank for more.

Bernie wasn't to be outdone. "Maybe it started from static electricity. You know if electricity don't move it builds up a powerful heat."

Blanchard grimaced and rolled his eyes. "Afraid not. We think somebody intentionally set the fire. That's why we called it arson." He spoke slow and deliberate, like someone trying to explain nuclear physics to a group of morons. He also motioned to Hank to keep the beer coming.

"Now Alex, how can you say you know who lit that fire? Did you see someone light it?"

"I know who lit that fire, not because I seen someone light it, but because of what I seen beforehand." He grinned at everyone, took out his tobacco, laboriously extracted a paper and slowly rolled a lopsided cigarette. Scratching a wooden match on the bottom of the table, he lit up, took a deep drag, tilted back in his chair and drank another bottle of beer. Again, Alex grinned at his audience.

Penhallurick leaned forward. He'd had enough. "Stop flapping your gums, old man. Who lit the goddam fire? Just what did you see?" he demanded.

Alex sucked in more of the thick smoke and exhaled through his nose. Moving his head close to Blanchard's, he pointed and whispered through the smoke, "Why, it was Blind Clarence Archer, sitting right over there. He lit that fire!" As he spoke, the cigarette bobbed up and down in the corner of his mouth and ashes dropped on the terrycloth.

Blanchard waved futilely at the smoke surrounding him. "How do you know it was Clarence, Alex?" He'd lowered his voice and his tone was conspiratorial. Penhallurick motioned for more beer.

"How do I know? How do I know?" repeated Alex. "I'll tell you how I know. It couldn't have been more than a week before the fire, I saw Blind Clarence, that's him right over there ... I saw Blind Clarence walking down the street with a match in his hand."

Hank arrived laughing. He was carrying another round for the table.

❦ ❦

"It's going to be hot for the funeral. Will you have another cold one, sir?"

Startled, I looked up. Hank Junior was setting another beer on the table. "Why yes, thank you. Say, I was wondering ... did they ever figure out who burned down the Pool elevator twenty-five years ago?"

"Why, yes sir, they did. They decided it was kids setting off firecrackers over by the railway tracks."

GOING BLIND *in* TUCKAHOE

I was fourteen that year, firmly wedged in the confusing and dangerous gap between childhood innocence and adult knowledge. Confusing, because puberty short-circuits rational thought. Dangerous, because both good and evil sometimes slip through this adolescent gap and take up residence at opposite ends of a soul.

At such times the mind of a boy may forever become wasted space where lies vie with truth, where twisted, narrow creeds replace innocence and where dogma overshadows the brilliance of self-discovery. This is when youth needs role models, older guides who have successfully travelled the tricky freeway between guilt and self-assurance, between late night fantasy and a mature relationship.

I didn't know it then, but my guides were still looking for the on-ramp. At this critical juncture, the role of mentor and sage pertaining to all things hormonal was filled by our hired man on the farm near Tuckahoe, my older cousin, Isaac. He taught me theory. Practical applications were the domain of Abigail Davies, wife of Reverend Jason Davies, pastor at Tuckahoe's Singing Evangelist Holy Gospel Church.

Although Reverend Davies was new at his job, he already had a reputation for being the most righteous hellfire and Holy Ghost preacher Tuckahoe had ever seen. Using his piety like a wedge, he inserted himself into the lives of everyone in town.

He even went into the Cenotaph Hotel Beer Parlour and lectured the regulars about the evils of alcohol. He was persuasive. He talked Old Charley Mergenfelter away from his Saturday night beer table and into a pew on Sunday mornings . . . and Charley had been sitting at that table for over fifty years! He collected parishioners from all the other churches in town. Even Mom went to see what all the fuss was about, and then she made me attend Sunday school!

It wasn't just Reverend Davies that got folks' attention. His wife, Abigail, did too. She made no bones about the fact that living in Tuckahoe hadn't been her first choice and that being a preacher's wife hadn't been her choice either. She did help around the church but refused to act like the other ministers' wives. Rumour had it that she had helped a number of male members of Reverend Davies' congregation break the Seventh Commandment. She told Lydia Mergenfelter, "If God or my husband or anyone else figures I'm going to spend the rest of my life eating tiny sandwiches in this dump, they're drinking from the wrong jug. This place is so boring, I cheat in solitaire to break the monotony."

She was a looker and half the Reverend's age. She had a way of tossing her black hair and pushing her body forward so she was always aimed at the horizon. Most days she wandered around town in pants that showed every nook and cranny. On top, she stuck out more than the awning on Louie's Cafe. She bothered me a lot.

The worst was in church one Sunday. She wore a tight dress and sat in a pew across from where I was with Mom and Dad. When she crossed her legs her skirt hiked up until I could see the tops of her nylons. It got me going so much I couldn't get up when the service was over. I had to sit there and talk to Reverend Davies.

"It's gratifying to have someone so young stay back after church," he said. "Is there anything in particular you want to ask me, Obbie?"

"Oh . . . no sir. I . . . I . . . was just interested in your sermon."

"Good for you, young man. It's never too soon to learn how God deals with drinkers and fornicators. As I said in the sermon, He turned Lot into a pillar of salt, but most sinners will burn in everlasting hell. If you're ever tempted, Obbie, just come into the light of the Lord."

"Yes sir," I said, trying not to look at Abigail. She was behind him with an expression on her face like our cat has when she's teasing a mouse to death. Like I said, she bothered me a lot.

Isaac was another matter. He was Mom's nephew and just out of the army. My dad wasn't his biggest fan. They were as different as horseradish and strawberries. Dad only gave him the job because Mom insisted. "I'm not in favour of hiring that loud-mouthed beer tub," he told her. "He can't be your relative. He doesn't know which leg his left foot is on. Are you sure he wasn't adopted?"

✄ ✄

My father and mother came from families that arrived in this country as a result of the Scottish Clearances — good, solid people whose real religion was hard work. The first commandment in our home was Thou Shalt Not Shirk, closely followed by Thou Shalt Not Display Emotion.

Things considered indecent or salacious had a low profile because they detracted from the three main purposes in life: backbreaking toil, education, and the intake of scotch whiskey. This holy trinity was deemed complete, since proper adherence to it covered all bases. Work kept one physically sound, education kept one's mind flexed and active, and scotch was the perfect lubricant for friction in one's soul.

An appropriate cause could always be determined for any effect. If a man was short, it was because he smoked when he was young. There was a suitable character flaw at the root of anyone's misfortune. If it wasn't obvious, then lack of piety was invoked. Just as work, education, and scotch brought desired effects, so too, a proper attitude toward sex would lead a young man to the blissful state of marriage, home and family.

Sex was, officially anyway, the expression of married love — to be engaged in for the purpose of procreation only — a righteous, if somewhat leaky, umbrella hastily thrown open whenever the rainfall of reality threatened to dampen the overcoat protecting Reverend Davies' fantasies. It never worked, but it took his mind off the fact that his moral fabric was getting soaked.

I never questioned any of this until the inevitable day that reality drizzled on my parade. It happened in the schoolyard after I flattened Leonard Cleary at home plate, scoring the winning run in our noon baseball game.

He was older than me and he turned the equation of my existence upside down when he yelled, "Robertson, you little shit! Don't get too big for your long johns. From what I hear, if it wasn't for the back seat of a thirty-nine Ford and a bottle of homebrew, you wouldn't exist!"

I didn't know exactly what he was driving at, so I asked my mother when I got home — a cause that brought about the effect of making my mouth taste like soap for the rest of the day. Her face got red and she warned me I must never ask that again. She took it so seriously that I knew there was truth in the allegation. To this day I find it humbling to know that the root cause of my existence can be traced to fermented potato peelings.

Inquiring about teenage stirrings and emotions was out of the question. My parents would sooner have spent a forty-below night on Arctic tundra than expound on any adolescent condition, let alone the one most perplexing: the sexual one.

I don't know how girls handled the dilemma, but boys usually turned to each other for information. Now, getting a male juvenile to admit he doesn't know something is a little like getting drunk with the pope — it's possible, but it just isn't going to happen. As a consequence, most of the lore sloshing around in our immature minds made a sea of misinformation. Deep down we knew that. So one of the stages in our research into all things prurient was verification, usually done by asking an older brother, or, if you were lucky enough to have one, a hired man.

There was another source of information, of which we were all sceptical. This was the ubiquitous book, the one every mother left lying around for her son to find. Ideally, he would read it and not ask embarrassing questions. The book would just appear one day at the foot of your bed or folded into your Saturday night dress-up shirt. It always had a title like *A Christian's Guide to Telling Your Children About Sex*, or *Speaking Plainly about the Birds and the Bees*.

The book was filled with useful advice such as, "Sex should only be engaged in for the purpose of having children," or, "If lewd thoughts are trying to enter your mind, think about other things, such as sports or a hobby."

I tried it. Once, in school, I started getting lewd thoughts about Eva Mae Parker, one of the girls in my class. I was the goalie for the Tuckahoe Terriers hockey team so I started thinking about our next game. I pretended I had a shutout going when I happened to glance over to the penalty box. There was Eva Mae standing beside it — with no clothes on!

The following week, during our game against Stoneboat Creek, I kept looking over to see if she was there. I let in five goals in the first period alone. We lost nine to three.

🦗 🦗

Isaac told me a lot about what happens between guys and girls — he didn't leave out details. When he got wound up I could almost see the naked women he carried on with when he was in the army. To tell the truth, I thought of nothing else. His stories almost wrecked my life. It would have been easier to pass algebra than stop thinking about girls. Even Coach Nelson figured it out. He told me I'd better choose between *nookie* and the *net* or he'd find himself a new goalie.

Mostly I thought about Eva Mae. She was different than other girls. The word was she went all the way, and she was one of the few girls in school who didn't stuff her bra with Kleenex. But she wouldn't give me the time of day. She only went out with guys who had their driver's license.

"I know, Obbie," Isaac said. "When you're hard, horny and hoping, it seems like forever, but don't worry 'cause it's going to happen in its own GeeVee time."

But geez, when I laid there in the middle of the night and thought about Eva Mae all naked, it felt so sweet and tingly I thought I'd explode right there in bed. I knew better than to do anything about it though, because Reverend Davies took all us boys out after Sunday school and told us about Onan dropping his seeds. He said God killed Onan, but because we were kids, He'd probably just make us go blind if we dropped our seeds.

I told Isaac about the Reverend's warning but he just laughed and said, "If Reverend Davies is right, the company that makes those white canes should be bigger than General Motors. GeeVee, Obbie, maybe the good Reverend should try dropping a few seeds. I doubt if it'd affect his eyesight, but it just might change his outlook."

The next thing I knew he was wound up in a story. "Actually, kid," he said, "the only time I ever heard of anybody getting in trouble for *doin' what comes natcherly* was back in basic training in the army. A prairie boy named Calvin Sump was caught playing with himself in the shower and they hauled him up on charge."

"Geez, Isaac. What happened to him?"

"I don't rightly remember. I think he had to do a bunch of extra duty. He was found guilty even though he had a good defence. He said God gave it to him, it was his and he was entitled to wash it as fast as he wanted. The only other thing I remember is, from then on, he was known as Pump Sump."

I looked at him but I couldn't tell if he was pulling my leg or not. He just lit up a roll-your-own and gazed at the clouds.

Anyway, I thought about it a lot. The way I figured, if I didn't want to end up blind or dead, something had to happen fast.

Actually, something did happen. Being ancient, Charley Mergenfelter just couldn't get used to his new diet of hymn singing instead of beer drinking. He expired right there in his pew one morning, while everyone was praying. Folks just thought he was asleep, so it wasn't 'til everybody got up to go home they figured out something was wrong.

Me and my parents got to his funeral early. We sat and looked at Charley lying in his coffin. Someone had put a tie on him. His face seemed a little smug. It crossed my mind that his timing in joining Reverend Davies' church had been perfect, like butting your cigarette just before your old man walks around the corner.

Abigail came down the aisle. She asked Mom if she could borrow me to lift some boxes she needed moved in the church annex, where they were going to feed everybody after they came back from burying Charley.

Mom wasn't pleased. I was dressed in my best and she didn't want me to get dirt on my good clothes. I went anyway. Reverend Davies wasn't in the annex. Abigail said he was consoling Charley's widow.

I lifted the boxes for her. When I turned to go, she held out a plate of goodies and asked me if I'd like something.

"Sure," I said, and took a cookie.

She stood and watched while I munched it. I started to get bothered. She had on a black dress with buttons down the front. Her fingers played with the buttons, undoing a few and then doing them back up. I finished my cookie and she offered me another. Then she poured me a glass of juice. When she handed it to me the juice splashed on my good shirt and pants. She said she was sorry and started to brush away the stain on my pants. Pretty soon she quit brushing and started rubbing.

All sorts of things happened. My brain shrunk to nothing and other parts started growing. My whole body got stiffer than Old Charley and I couldn't breathe. Then, as cool as you please, she leaned over and kissed me full on the mouth.

My mouth was full of cookies. I didn't know what to do. She leaned back and asked me if I liked it. I couldn't answer on account of my mouth being full. She was up against me and still rubbing. I was right on the verge of going blind and there was nothing I could do. That's when she decided to have a conversation.

"I bet a good looking young fellow like you has lots of girlfriends. Do any of them do this to you?" She rubbed faster.

My mouth was still full of cookies. She said, "Never mind. Let's see if I can guess. Do they ever do this?" She quit rubbing and squeezed me with her hand. Things went black. I thought

God was making me blind on the spot. Then I realised I'd shut my eyes.

"How about this?" she asked, and kissed me again. I finally swallowed the cookie. It tasted funny. Salt! I was turning into a pillar of salt! Then she put her tongue in my mouth. It was hard to breathe. Things got hazy again. She pushed herself against me and I felt her fingers undoing my pants.

"Why, what's this?" she asked. "Does me talking about your girlfriends get you excited? We have to do something about it, Obbie. You can't walk back into church like this." She pushed down my trousers and I could feel cool air where her hand wasn't covering me.

In the back of my mind I was scared. What if Reverend Davies came in? What if Mom came looking for me? Then I heard singing and I knew the funeral had started. She kissed me again and backed me across the room, until I sat down hard on a chair by the wall. She leaned over, straddling me, her tongue still in my mouth. She had her fingers wrapped around me like she was scared it was going to come off and run away. Her hand moved me around until she had me where she wanted. Then she lowered herself. I felt like I was going to explode. She started to move up and down, and I closed my eyes.

Reverend Davies was into the hell-fire part of his sermon. "Beware the warm, enticing softness of the devil. If it envelops you, you must move. MOVE YOURSELF! DON'T BE AFRAID. LET YOURSELF COME! COME INTO THE LIGHT OF THE LORD!"

She quit kissing me and bounced up and down, faster and faster. I opened my eyes. Her head was thrown back. Behind her, Jesus was staring down at me from a cross on the far wall.

Suddenly she started jerking and screaming, "OH GOD! OH GOD! OH GOD!"

I heard Reverend Davies shout, "HALLELUJAH!"

I felt my eyesight draining away. God had struck me blind but I didn't care. Going blind was fantastic.

Later, when everyone had left to plant Charley, I sneaked out the back. Isaac was standing there smoking. "Ain't you going to the graveyard?" I asked.

"Oh no," he said. "I hate funerals. I been out here the whole time."

Then he got a funny grin on his face. "How's your eyesight, kid?" he asked.

Twisting *and* Bending
Like *a* Politician's Speech

We were sitting beside a dry slough, washing ash from our throats with cold beer. Isaac was fingering burn holes in his old army uniform. A breeze skittered across the black field, fanning small flames dancing at the edge of the break. A whitetail deer, confused by the fire, stood in the slough, its perked-up ears visible in the tall grass. Wispy columns of smoke rose, twisting and bending like a politician's speech.

A river of dust followed a car down the road and spread out in the blue sky. The car slowed and came to a stop beside the field. I could make out white letters on the door and there was a red light on top. Two men got out and walked toward us. One was Constable Dave; the other was a Mountie.

Isaac grabbed me by the shoulder. "GeeVee Keereist, Obbie. Keep your mouth shut about me being here. I gotta disappear for awhile."

Carrying his beer, he eased into the tall grass. The whitetail flicked its ears and disappeared. I stuck my bottle in my belt, under my jacket, and went to meet them.

Constable Dave is a big man. Three days a week he's Tuckahoe's town cop. The other days he pumps gas down at Mac's Garage. The town hasn't got around to buying him a uniform, so he puts on his gas jockey outfit for both jobs. I could tell it was one of his police days: he was wearing sunglasses.

"Hello, Obbie," he said. "You looking after this fire all alone?"

I looked behind me. Isaac was nowhere in sight. "Yes sir, I am," I said.

"Obbie, this is Corporal Van Imschoot of the RCMP. He wants to talk to your cousin Isaac. Is he around?"

"No, he isn't. Is something wrong?"

"Yes, something's wrong. Do you know where he is?"

"No. I haven't seen him. Mom and Dad went to Saskatoon to visit my grandparents. Maybe Isaac went with them. If not, he's gone to different pastures."

Corporal Van Imschoot pulled a notebook from his pocket. He didn't take his eyes off me, even when he was writing. I didn't like lying, but I had no choice. Isaac had asked me to keep quiet, so there wasn't much else I could do. At least the part about Mom and Dad going to Saskatoon was true.

Dave took off his sunglasses and pointed them at me. "You sure, Obbie? You mean your folks don't mind you out here all alone, burning stubble? I don't think so. I know your dad. He'd never let a fourteen-year-old do this job alone. You sure Isaac ain't around?" He gazed around the field.

"Why, no, sir. My dad doesn't know I'm burning stubble. He was going to do it when he got back. The wind was right so I thought I'd surprise him. I did the firebreak yesterday and I lit backfires this morning. Why are you looking for Isaac, anyway?" The more lies I told, the easier they came.

Corporal Van Imschoot stopped taking notes. "We want to talk to him about some unfinished business he has with the government. When's the last time you saw him?"

"Geez, sir, I don't know . . . two or three days ago, I guess."

"Do you have any idea where he might be? Does he have a girl, or is there a friend's place where he might be staying? Are there other relatives nearby?"

"No sir, no relatives besides us. Why did you say you wanted to see him?"

"Sorry son, it's between him and the government. I'll leave you a phone number. Give me a call when he comes back, okay?"

"Yes, sir. I'll phone if I see him."

Dave looked at me funny. He still wasn't buying. I walked around, to get them to turn, so they wouldn't be facing the slough. The bottle slid down the inside of my pant leg and stopped at my ankle. Beer splashed and wet my leg. I glanced down. White foam was running over my left boot.

Fire had crept into the long grass where Isaac was hiding. I talked fast to keep their attention off my boot and away from the slough. "I'm sorry I can't help. I don't know where he is. He might have gone with Mom and Dad, or he might be at one of his girlfriend's in Stoneboat Creek. He has a few over there, but I don't know where they live."

Behind the policemen, Isaac stood up and started to run. The flames were close to him. I could see smoke coming from the seat of his pants. He was slapping his rear end as he came out the far side of the slough and made for the edge of the field. I kept talking.

"You know, he might be staying at the Cenotaph Hotel. Sometimes, if he gets a snootful, he takes a room."

Corporal Van Imschoot saw me looking past him and turned around. Heavy smoke hid Isaac as he crossed the fire break and disappeared into the bush at the edge of the field. The deer bounded out of the tall grass and ran right by us. I breathed easier and kicked dust over my left boot.

The Mountie turned back. "Okay, son. Phone us if you hear from him. Thanks for your time." He motioned to the burning slough. "If I was you, I'd keep an eye on this fire awhile. It ain't all out yet and you don't want it spreading to your neighbour's. By the way, you've spilled something on your boot."

"Yes sir, I'll stick around." I said.

They headed for their car. I waited until they were driving down the road before I undid my pants and got the beer bottle.

⚐   ⚑

The dust trail from the police car faded. I walked to the edge of the field, keeping an eye on the road in case they came back. Isaac was sitting under a chokecherry bush, eating berries and drinking his beer. He grinned at me. "Damn, Obbie. I burned my ass in that GeeVee slough. Have they gone?"

"Yeah, they're gone. But I had to lie like crazy. Why are they looking for you? The Mountie said you and the government had unfinished business. Did you do something bad?"

"I guess you could call it unfinished business," he said. "Me and the army just didn't get along that well ... you know ... like Protestants and Catholics."

"But what's the problem, Isaac? You've got discharge papers, don't you?"

"Uuh ... not exactly. I mean ... they were coming. It's just that I left before they got there."

"How long before they got there? You're AWOL, aren't you?"

"About six months. Yeah, I guess I am AWOL. I couldn't wait. I done some things the army didn't look kindly on, so I had to light out early. Your dad's farm seemed as good a place as any to lay low. KeeReist, don't rat on me, Obbie."

"Okay, Isaac. I won't say anything, but what kind of things did you do?"

"It's a long story, but if you want to hear it, I'll try and cut it short."

I had to grin. He never stopped talking as long as someone was listening. Cutting his story short wasn't going to happen.

"It all started with a small disagreement I had with my sergeant," he said.

"What kind of disagreement?"

"Well, he never seemed pleased with my performance during drill on the parade square."

"What was wrong? Couldn't you march in step?"

"Of course I could march in step, kid. I just wasn't as crisp as some of the other guys."

"What do you mean, 'not as crisp'? What did he say to you?"

"If you gotta know, he said I marched like a pregnant rhinoceros with a club foot, and when I protested, he put me on extra duty, evenings and weekends."

"You didn't go AWOL over that, did you? It doesn't sound too serious to me."

"Oh no, Obbie. It wasn't that. It was what happened later."

"What happened, Isaac?"

"It was this way. I got sent out on a Saturday to weed General Gordon's garden. He was the commanding officer and lived in a big house just off the base."

"What did you do, steal some carrots?"

"No, I didn't steal no carrots! Don't be a smartass, kid." He took a swig from his bottle.

"Okay, I'm sorry. What happened?"

He popped some chokecherries in his mouth, chewed them and spit out the stones. "When I got there, the general wasn't home, just his wife was. She was sunning herself in the backyard, right beside the garden, wearing almost nothing for a bathing suit, and KeeReist, she was one well-built woman, I tell you. I started in weeding, but before I knew it we were talking and she was pouring drinks. The whole afternoon just slipped away."

"So, that's how you got in trouble. You didn't do your job, you didn't weed the garden."

"No, Obbie. That's not it. No one found out about the garden. No, one thing just led to another. Pretty soon, she was picking me up whenever the general was away. She'd drive by and I'd hop in her car about a block from the main gate. She called one day when I was on duty. I sneaked away and she picked me up. We did what we usually did when the general was away. She lit up a smoke and we drove around for awhile and talked. Then she pulled the car into their garage and I closed the door."

He stopped talking and his eyes got dreamy, as if he was caught up in the memory.

"What happened then, Isaac? Did you go in the house?"

"No, we didn't. We started going at it, hot and heavy, right there in the car. Pretty soon we'd shucked our clothes and crawled into the back seat. GeeVee, we got so interested in what we were doing, I didn't notice the coal from her cigarette had fallen off while we were still in the front. Just like that, the car was filled with smoke and our clothes were burning in the front seat. We scrambled out in a hurry. The fire was too far gone to even think about putting it out. The flames were everywhere in a minute, outside the car, and burning in newspapers stacked by the wall."

"Geez, Isaac, did you get burned? What about her?"

"We hung on as long as we could, but the smoke got so thick we had to open the door and run outside. A lot of people, neighbours and folks just passing, were standing in the front yard watching the smoke pour out of the roof. One of the ones watching was the general. He looked shocked when the door opened and we came racing out without a stitch on."

"So, that's how you got in trouble? You burned down the general's garage?"

"Well, not exactly. You see, the fire spread to the house and burned it down, too."

"Holy smoke, Isaac! No wonder you had to run. You burned down the general's house. What happened to the fire department? Didn't they come?"

"Oh, yeah, they sure did. The whole fire crew from the base showed up . . . on foot! All of them, without the fire truck or the pumper, so they couldn't fight the fire. That's why the GeeVee house burned to the ground."

"That sounds stupid. Why did they walk? Why didn't they bring the fire truck?"

"Well, that's the real reason I left. I was Duty Driver that day and the keys for the fire truck were in my pants that burned up in the front seat of the car."

He put his head back, tipped his bottle, and shook it for the last drop. Then he smirked, wiped his mouth on his sleeve, and lit a cigarette. "So you see, kid, today ain't the first time I burned my ass running from a fire."

☙ ❧

Corporal Van Imschoot stepped from behind the chokecherry bush. Constable Dave was behind him. They walked over and lifted Isaac by his shoulders. The Mountie looked at me. "It was the beer on your boot, Obbie. No fourteen year-old would be sitting in a burning field drinking by himself. It was your face too. You're not a good liar."

The whitetail broke from the bush, swerved by us, leapt the fence and bounded away across the neighbour's field. Isaac grinned at me. "Let that be a lesson, Obbie. That fence is nothing for a deer, but a pregnant rhinocerous with a club foot would never make it."

ROBERTA'S ALL-STARS

Roberta made us up in her head. She said we were a baseball team, but we were really an idea — an idea that became a family. Without her there would have been no All-Stars. And without the All-Stars, half of us would be in jail by now. It's strange when you think about it. Roberta was forty years old and she didn't know the first thing about baseball, but she was our manager. When she died, she still didn't know that, in baseball, stealing isn't a crime.

🙖 🙖

It all started in the baked brown yard in front of Roberta's house. I was hitting some lazy grounders to Buck, and a couple of the guys were pretending to help Roberta in the garden when Constable Dave, Tuckahoe's town cop, came roaring up the dirt road to Roberta's farm at about a hundred per with his red light flashing and his siren blowing, like he'd just learned Jesse James was hiding in the hayloft. There was a huge crease down the side of his black police car.

As soon as the car stopped he jumped out and yelled, "I'm here for Buck. That dumb S.O.B. has really done it this time."

Roberta was standing in the garden holding her apron away from her. It was half-full of green peas. Dave stomped straight into the garden, tramping on her prize dahlias. The dust from his car spread across the yard and settled on white sheets hanging from a line stretched between the house and a stunted poplar bent over from the weight of the week's washing.

She opened her mouth, but Dave wasn't finished. "This is the last straw. Go get the little jerk. If I got to go lookin', so-help-me-God, I'll shoot him. I'm going to charge him. He stole my car and put a big dent in it."

Roberta dropped her apron and the peas scattered in the dirt. She put her hands on her hips and her shoulders came up. "There's some mistake, Dave." She pushed back a strand of brown hair. "Buck wouldn't steal a car. It's not like him, and Dave, you're standing in my flowers."

He backed away. "The hell it isn't like him. I found his green jacket in the ditch, right beside the car. I'm putting him away this time."

She couldn't have weighed ninety pounds. Constable Dave was almost two feet taller than she was, and a whole lot heavier. I thought of David and Goliath.

She stepped gingerly over the peas. Dave retreated but kept talking. "If he didn't take it, show me his jacket. What do you think I got here, Roberta — the Queen of England's fur coat?" He held out the jacket like it had a bad smell.

Roberta looked shocked. We crowded in close but she frowned us out of the garden. "Why, that *is* his jacket! He told me he lost it. Whoever found it must have stolen your car. But you can't take Buck. He's my oldest boy. The kids look up to him. We need him here on the farm."

Constable Dave rolled a scowl over his face and yelled through it. "What do you mean I can't take him? He stole my car. I gotta take him."

Her smile soaked up his scowl as quick as a breeze eats mist off a mirror. "I doubt he stole anything, but even if he did, he's still a kid. Maybe he made a mistake. Can we pay for the damage to the car?"

Dave puffed himself up. "I ain't going to let you work something this time, Roberta. Somebody's got to set an example. You're running a crime school. I'm out here two, three times a week. Your boys are going wild. They only go to school half the time and they're in trouble the other half. I gotta do something. People expect me to crack down on these kids."

"No, Dave. I can't let you have Buck. How much will it cost to fix your car?"

"I already got an estimate — over two hundred dollars. It's gotta be fixed and paid right now."

She smiled at him again. "We don't have that kind of money, but with a little time we can come up with it."

Dave rolled his eyes and looked over her head at the sagging roof on the house. "With these kids, I'm sure you could, Roberta. Problem is, somebody would be missing two hundred dollars."

He shuffled his feet. Roberta didn't take her eyes off him. "Okay," he said, "it's against my better judgment, but I'll get the car fixed. The town will pay for it, but they'll want the money back. You got 'til the end of the month before I run the little crook in. Remember, he's old enough to go to jail. And Roberta, I'm sorry about the flowers."

⌇ ⌇

My name is Stevey Albertson. Roberta Ross had this beat-up farm next to ours. She had two boys of her own and a tribe of others nobody else wanted. She collected lost causes the way bums pick cigarette butts off the street. Nobody knew where Mr. Ross was, or if there ever had been a Mr. Ross.

My mom died when I was twelve and my dad was away a lot, so Roberta's became a second home for me and my kid brothers. She didn't try to be our mother. She just fed us and let us hang around.

Apart from us and her two kids, she looked after five other guys. They belonged to a woman named Margaret Angler who my dad hired to cook during harvest. Margaret made no secret that some of her boys had different fathers. "I figured hooking up with lots of men, one of 'em might turn out decent," she said. "So far my lifetime batting average is zero."

After harvest she left with one of the hired men. Only thing is, she forgot to take her kids.

The oldest was Buck and the youngest was Little Joe. Little Joe didn't talk. He'd gone to school for a couple of years before his mom took off. The teachers figured he was too dumb to learn anything so he didn't go anymore, but he could still print some words. Roberta bought him a pencil and scribbler and he practised in it. I looked at it one day. It was almost full. He'd written our names over and over on every page. He'd done pretty good, except he spelled Danny with one "n" and he changed Roberta into "Roberto".

Little Joe was ten, but he was so small folks thought he was younger. Buck told me Joe's dad beat him bad and that's when he quit talking. Buck was seventeen. The rest of us were in between Joe and Buck.

We must have been a handful. Our only interests were the creek under the bridge, mealtimes and baseball. If we couldn't swim in it, eat it, or hit it, we weren't interested. School and chores didn't enter the equation.

In summer we spent entire days playing ball and swimming. All of us, that is, except Little Joe. Sometimes he'd walk into the water up to his knees, but he'd just stand there and shiver before he turned around and trudged back to the farm. He never played baseball, either. He tried, but he was just too small and skinny. He couldn't hit and there was no way he could chase down a fly ball. Finally he gave up. While we played he sat on the side and printed our names in his scribbler.

Not one of us had stuck with a league or school team. Living on the farm, we rarely showed up for practice. The coaches thought we weren't serious so we always got dropped.

Baseball was our day world; finding trouble in town was what we did after dark. Roberta never lectured us. She believed if you kept a boy clean and his belly full, proper behaviour would show up one day, like mushrooms appear in manure piles.

᠅ ᠅

Constable Dave drove out of the yard mumbling to himself. Buck looked a little foolish. There was no doubt in anyone's mind that he'd taken the car. He'd done stuff like that before, but I couldn't understand why he hadn't said anything.

"Why did you do it?" I asked when we were alone. "Why did you take a cop car? You knew you'd never get away with it."

"I didn't take it, Stevey. I wasn't even out last night."

"Then who . . . " I stopped. "The jacket!" Little Joe was always wearing Buck's jacket.

He nodded. So Joe took the car. No wonder Buck had shut up. He didn't want to get Little Joe in trouble.

But somebody was going to be in trouble. Two hundred dollars was out of the question. After Dave left, Roberta called a meeting under the crippled poplar. Even though we jammed in close, there wasn't enough shade for all of us. "It might as well be two thousand," she said. "We might be able to raise fifty dollars if we sold our souls and robbed a bank." Some of the guys looked up when she mentioned robbing a bank, but Buck glared at them and they shut up.

It was a big problem. There was no doubt Constable Dave would run Buck in if we didn't come up with the money, and we only had a few weeks. Nobody had any ideas. It was depressing. We all just moped around. We even quit playing ball for a few days.

That was before Roberta spotted the poster at Louie's Cafe — an ad for Tuckahoe's annual summer fair. The Agricultural Society was putting up five hundred dollars, half as a gate prize to be drawn on the final evening. But the big news was they were putting up the other half as first prize in a baseball tournament.

We were swimming under the bridge. She came running down the hill waving the poster. "Do you think you have a shot at this?" she yelled.

The next morning we all went to the town office and watched Roberta pay the ten dollar fee. She signed the entry form as our manager and she filled in the team name as the All-Stars. "You're all stars to me," she explained.

The title must have gone to her head. She had us on the diamond as soon as the sun was up, and she made us stay there all day. Then we had to do chores. Swimming was out of the question. We worked so hard we had no energy to sneak into town.

She held nightly pep talks in the kitchen. "Doing your best is more important than winning," she said as she waved a mug of hot chocolate and brushed back disobedient strands of hair. "If you're good sports, God will keep Buck out of jail."

Ten pairs of eyes rolled up at the ceiling. "Yes, ma'am," Danny said. "We'll try our best."

🦅 🦅

There were eight teams entered. That meant we had to win two games to get to the final on Sunday. Our first game was

Saturday morning against the local high school, the Tuckahoe Tigers.

We watched the Spring City Gems get off their bus. They were tall and thin and didn't smile or joke — barnstormers who made a living going from tournament to tournament. "They're all business," Buck said. "They look like they need to win to eat."

Me and Buck were our only pitchers. I wasn't good, but I might get us by the high school team. We had to save Buck for later. He was super on the mound, short and squat like a tree stump. He had a soaring fastball that batters popped up, and an overhand curve that faded like a childhood dream. We were the only ones who could hit him. We'd swung on him so long we had him memorised.

Buck would have blown out the high school, but I didn't have speed or much of anything else. You could time my fastball with a sundial. Their pitcher was all power, which was good for us. After the hours we'd spent hitting Buck, nobody could scare us by throwing hard.

Roberta sat on the bench, but she left the details of the game to Buck. She confined herself to dealing with the overall strategy. When their star slugger came to the plate, she called time and came out to the mound. "You don't have to worry about this batter," she told me. "I know his parents and both of them wear glasses. Save your arm, Stevey."

I reared back, fired as hard as I could, and struck out Bumphead Lyzewski on three pitches. Roberta smiled and gave me a thumbs up.

The guys bailed me out lots, and we ended up winning eleven to eight. It wasn't great, but it was enough.

The afternoon game was tougher. The Stoneboat Creek Swallows were big and swung lumber like toothpicks. They had a left-hander who carried his cap about seven feet off the ground. When he threw, his hand was in your face. Buck held them to three hits. We didn't hit at all, but a walk and a couple of errors gave us a one run lead and we managed to hang on.

During the games Little Joe sat on our bench, but he only paid attention when Buck was at bat. The rest of the time he snuggled up against Roberta and wrote in his scribbler. It was full, so he erased each name before he reprinted it.

I talked to Buck while we looked at the draw sheet. "You ready for tomorrow?" I asked.

The Gems had blown out the teams on their side of the draw. If they scared Buck, he didn't show it. "Don't worry, Stevey. We can handle them," he said.

On Sunday the sun was warm enough to make folks hurry with their ice cream cones. A breeze rustled leaves in the maples lining the fairground. We arrived early. Ball players didn't have to pay admission. That meant we didn't get a chance to fill out an entry for the grand prize. The whole town was out, so there wasn't much chance of winning the draw anyway.

We were nervous and it showed. The Gems got their first two batters around, so we had a meeting on the mound to give Buck some encouragement. Danny told him, "You better start throwin' good, or your dumb ass is going to be locked away 'til your pecker falls off from lack of use."

The encouragement seemed to work. He settled down, and from then on nobody got past first. We went to the bottom of the ninth down the two runs.

I was lead-off, not because I hit better than the other guys but because I could get hit better than they could. By crowding, I could take a ball when I had to, and if I ever had to, this was the time.

I put my toes on the plate and leaned over, so no self-respecting pitcher would have any choice but to push me back. It didn't take long. He threw a high hard one at my head and

I ducked out of the box. I didn't mind getting hit to keep Buck out of jail, but I wasn't going to get my brain scrambled for him. I stepped back in and crowded up again. Sure enough, he threw the next one a little lower. I turned into the pitch and it hit me on the back of the shoulder. One on and nobody out.

Roberta called time and came over to make sure I was okay. "Buck says not to steal and I agree," she whispered. "Stealing's what got us in trouble in the first place."

Then she turned toward the mound and waved her finger at the pitcher. "You did that on purpose," she shouted. "Don't you dare hit one of my boys again, or you'll have me to deal with."

Danny was up. No one could bunt like he could. He sacrificed me to second, only it turned out to be no sacrifice. He beat the throw to first. Now we had two on. We needed a swat. My brother, Jimmy, was next and he hit a short fly to right field. Normally I wouldn't have tagged, but there was a lot at stake. So when the ball hit the fielder's mitt, I was gone. I must have surprised him, because he threw it a mile wide and pulled the third baseman off the bag. I was safe by twenty feet. Danny went to second.

The crowd got into it. Folks cheered and I heard somebody yell, "Not bad for delinquents." Roberta pressed her lips together and stared straight ahead.

Our next guy grounded to first. Two out, but Buck was up. He never had trouble putting wood on the ball. They called time and had a meeting. I thought they might walk him. Instead they pushed their outfielders to the fence and backed their infield off the line.

Buck did exactly what we knew he'd do: he dropped one down. I squeezed home, sliding through the plate before a stunned catcher even had the ball. He turned and threw wild to first. Buck was already there. The ball sailed over the first baseman's head. Danny came chugging toward home carrying the tie. Their right fielder backed up the play and he threw a perfect strike. Danny slid and the catcher reached for him. The umpire yelled, "OUT," and jerked his thumb.

We'd lost! We'd pulled up one run short!

You never saw such a sad bunch. I was ashamed. I couldn't look anyone in the eye. I felt like I'd let Roberta down. Buck's face looked like he was already in jail. There were tears in Little Joe's eyes. He trudged away carrying his scribbler.

Most of the guys walked back to the farm. I went and sat in the stands. No one was around. I saw Roberta and some other folks heading to the outdoor stage for the fireworks and closing ceremonies.

The disappearing sun was making long shadows when I saw Little Joe walking alone across the infield. He came over, took my hand and pulled me toward the stage. I didn't feel like looking at fireworks, but I figured if Joe wanted to see them I'd go with him. We watched exploding red pinwheels and shooting rockets. It didn't make me feel any better.

The last green star-shower dissolved in the black sky and the applause died away. The mayor put a cardboard box on the stage and then heaved himself up beside it. He picked up a microphone. "Thank you all for making this the best Tuckahoe Fair ever," he shouted into the crowd.

I started home. It sure hadn't been the best fair as far as we were concerned. Joe tugged my arm but I shrugged him off. He stopped and looked back, torn between following me and staying until the end of the show. I kept going. Joe knew the way; he'd walked it before.

I could hear the Mayor behind me. "Ladies and Gentlemen, the winner of the Tuckahoe Fair Grand Prize is . . . excuse me,

I'm having trouble making this out. It looks like . . . yes it is
. . . it's Roberta Ross. Roberta, come up and get your two-
hundred and fifty dollars."

I couldn't believe it! I ran back; Little Joe was ahead of me.
He hugged Roberta, jumped up and down, and ran circles
around her. Everyone yelled and cheered. The mayor came
down off the stage to meet Roberta. When he threw his arms
around her he dropped the folded paper he'd drawn from the
box. After they moved away I went over and picked it up.

I waited 'til everyone left and then I sneaked up and looked
in the box on the stage. No one paid any attention to me. I only
went through twenty or thirty of the folded pieces of paper.
Every one was printed in pencil and they all had the same
name: Roberto Ross.

❧ ❧

Everyone was back for Roberta's funeral. We stood under the
poplar beside the old house. It wasn't scrawny anymore. It
reached to the sky, straight and tall, with enough shade for all
of us. There were tears on Buck's cheeks and he seemed a
million miles away. Someone tapped my shoulder. Joe stood
behind me with his wife and baby girl. There were no tears on
his cheeks. He grinned. "She was a good manager," he said. "We
all won."

The ESSENCE *of a* MAN

From the beginning, Harold Montain was different than other folks. Most agreed he was destined for things far greater than could be found in our little town. To look at him you couldn't tell. He had blue eyes, freckles and a stubborn cowlick on the crown of his blond head. Like a plain package that hides its contents, the envelope enclosing Harold forecast nothing extraordinary. His behaviour was something else. He was a small lad who never sat still. Some called him precocious. The truth is he was curious. He never stopped asking questions. He wanted to know the why, when, where and who of everything. His favourite expression was, "How come?" From the time he could talk, "Howcum Harold" spent his days quizzing anyone who would take the time to answer.

"How come the sun comes up?"

"How come a rooster knows when the sun is going to come up?"

"How come we look at a clock to know when the sun is going to come up?"

"How come a rooster is smarter than us?"

His eyes shone when he asked a question and never blinked while he waited for the answer. The questions didn't stop as he got older.

"How come I can't see my own eyes, except in a mirror?"

"Does a mirror look the same when you're not looking into it?"

"If your left side is your right in a mirror, how come we're not upside down in it?"

His parents were ordinary people who worked hard and paid their bills. Only one trait distinguished them from their neighbours: permanent harried looks. Most of Howcum's questions were beyond them and he frustrated their efforts to distract him.

His father bought him a baseball glove.

"Why?" he asked.

His mother brought home a book for stamp collecting.

"To what end?" he enquired.

They dreamed of the day he would meet a nice girl, get married and settle down. Perhaps they would gain a daughter and lose the stress. But, even as a boy, the subject of girls raised more questions.

"How come girls are made of sugar and spice and everything nice?"

"How come boys are made of snakes and snails and puppy dog tails?"

"How come they're different?"

To say Howcum had a thirst for learning is an understatement, like saying that Romulus and Remus dabbled in city planning. At school he gulped down knowledge. His questions were unending and unanswerable, and he waited for answers with a wide-eyed expression his teachers took for insolence. Embarrassed and perplexed, they learned to sidestep Howcum's queries as deftly as one skirts a drunk's dinner on a sidewalk. When he finished high school, a party was held in the staff room to celebrate his impending departure. His class elected him valedictorian, an honour he deserved as the first

Tuckahoe male to finish high school, and an honour he received because no one else wanted it.

On graduation night the auditorium was strung with coloured streamers and packed with pride and anticipation. Mr. Armshank, the principal, was trapped in a hall closet. He'd slipped in earlier for a cigarette. He felt that smoking in public did not set a good example for students. Now, there were people in the hall and he couldn't come out. He was a tall, brooding man with too little padding on his backbone to absorb the stress that was eating its way from his belly. Everything seemed beyond his control. He'd always dealt with Howcum on a one-to-one basis. Graduation night was different. Lord knows what the boy would say. He took a nervous drag on his cigarette and thought about his first encounter, twelve years earlier. Howcum had been sent to the school office for insolence in class. The usual punishment was the strap.

"Why am I getting the strap?" Howcum asked.

"Because Mrs. Beangessner said you were insolent in class," he'd replied.

"How was I insolent?" Howcum asked.

"She says you asked questions."

"How did you find out I was insolent?"

"I asked Mrs. Beangessner why she sent you to see me."

"How come I get a strap for asking questions and you don't?" asked Howcum.

Mr. Armshank shuddered at the memory and peeked out the closet door. Folks were still standing in the hall talking. He sat down on the floor and lit another cigarette. Finally the hall emptied. Mr. Armshank came out of the closet. He went backstage and gave Howcum a sheet of paper. "When it's time for your speech, I want you to read this," he said. "There's no point in confusing everybody with a lot of questions."

The graduates filed onto the stage and the audience squirmed in the metal folding chairs. Some of the ladies examined their fingernails. Others glanced at Josephine Kinnear sitting primly on the stage, staring at the ceiling and tapping a white heeled shoe. In her taffeta and crinolines, it was difficult to tell if rumours about her being pregnant were true. A few men looked at the graduating girls and thought thoughts their wives had no idea they were thinking. Many parents gave thanks for the divine intervention that allowed one of their own to become a high school graduate. Two boys at the back slipped out for a smoke.

Howcum stepped to the podium and looked at his classmates, their parents, the teachers and all the invited guests. He pulled Mr. Armshank's speech from his pocket and started to read. "Classmates, parents, teachers and invited guests . . . as I walk down the hallowed halls for the last time and prepare to embark on life's highway, I think how far we've come these past twelve years . . . "

Mr. Armshank exhaled the breath he'd been holding. He was premature. Howcum folded the platitudes, put them back in his pocket, and continued speaking. Mr. Armshank felt a sudden urge to go to the toilet.

"Yes, we've come a long way, but from where? Where *do* we come from? Why don't we come from somewhere else? If we came from somewhere else, would others come from where we come from, or would they also come from somewhere else? Would they wonder where they came from? Would they care where I come from? If they don't care where I come from, should I care where they come from? If I don't care where they come from, does it *matter* where I come from?"

He paused. The audience relaxed. Some of the girls giggled. Mr. Armshank's urge abated, and then returned as Howcum took his second wind.

"When I think about the *where*, it makes me ask the *who*. Who am I? Why am I who I am and not someone else? If I was someone else, who would I be? Who would she be? Would she be me? If she was me, would she wonder why she wasn't somebody else, or why she was me instead of me? Would she wonder why she wasn't him?"

He paused for his third wind. The girls weren't giggling anymore. They were laughing hysterically. Mr. Armshank lit a cigarette, then threw it away when he realised he was on the stage. He stumbled toward the wing and headed to the toilet. But Howcum was winding down.

"Even though I haven't had one question answered at Tuckahoe High, I don't consider it a waste of time. The lack of answers has made me decide to go to university."

The assembled folk gasped. First high school, and now university . . . for a boy! It was unheard of. No boy had ever left Tuckahoe to go away to school, unless you counted Nick Fedorich attending a three day hog breeding seminar in Stoneboat Creek.

"I always knew he would amount to something," Lydia Mergenfelter whispered loudly to Reverend Davies at the back of the hall. "I just knew it in my bones. Why, he could be anything he wants to . . . a dentist, a veterinarian, or even a licensed mechanic. I guess we're really on the map now." Everyone in hearing range nodded in agreement.

❧ ☙

Howcum found university a step up from Tuckahoe High. He discovered philosophy and others who were interested in the same questions he was. He first astounded his professors and then moved past them as he mastered Plato, Schopenhauer, Kant, Wittgenstein, and Whitehead. His name spread beyond the university. His reputation became so formidable and his writings were so well-executed that conventional wisdom soon credited him with finding the answer to the meaning of human existence, explicating the basic nature of man, showing there is no difference between free will and determinism, defining truth and discovering the source of all knowledge.

One by one he dealt with the *isms* — pragmatism, empiricism, existentialism. Everything from aestheticism to positivism fell to the razor edge of his mental machete. Howcum was in his element. He revelled in intellectual froth. His effect on the world of philosophy was electric. It was like a five-star movie mystery — everyone waited to see what was coming next.

Then he discovered religion and a bunch more *isms*. Buddhism, Sihkism, Taoism, Catholicism, Mohammedism and Judaism were all poured into a metaphysical soup and stirred. In Howcum's opinion they sank. "Religion is a lazy man's philosophy. It's intellectual margarine," he stated in an interview with the Stoneboat Creek Sentinel.

When the interview was published, Reverend Davies, dressed in his most sanctimonious demeanour, paid a visit to Howcum's parents. He had work to do. Somewhere along the line, they must have reached an agreement with the devil.

Howcum's mother pointed out that Howcum hadn't mentioned the Singing Evangelist Holy Gospel Church and, if you didn't count Catholics, he hadn't even mentioned Christianity. Reverend Davies allowed as how she might be right and started planning his next Sunday sermon.

Though ideas were swimming through Howcum's pool, his social life was dry. He had a healthy interest in girls but not one had shown any interest in him. Most found his obsessions frightening, and the ones who didn't preferred to play carnal tic-tac-toe with the football team. So far, his sexual experience had been terribly one-sided.

His was more than hormonal curiosity. From the time he first heard about snakes and snails and sugar and spice, he'd pondered the difference between the sexes. Thus far his study had come to naught. Everything he'd learned applied equally to men and women.

For example, the famous dictum, *I think, therefore I am,* turned out to be useless. It supposedly proved the existence of the self. But Howcum knew many men who existed without hardly thinking at all. He also knew women who frequently engaged in thinking, yet claimed their lives were non-existent. He concluded that the difference between the sexes couldn't be based in thought and that nowhere in religion or philosophy would he find the explanation he sought.

As far as he could see, the things that made a man also made a woman. There were examples in both sexes of individuals who were fickle, greedy, truthful, sensitive, idealistic, cheerful, arrogant, humble, brilliant and perceptive. The answer was not an adjective. Sex couldn't be defined by a list of traits. Apart from the obvious, what made him a male and another member of the species a female? Was it possible he was just a woman with a handle? And what about the shapely undergraduate in his *Dialectical Materialism and the Evolution of Rock Music* tutorial (she called the class He-Ha, short for Hegel and Haley). Was she really just a guy with a bumpy chest? He knew it had to be more, but everything led to a dead end. He needed an idea, a research methodology, a hypothesis.

Howcum had one other talent besides philosophy: he was a decent cook and knew his way around a kitchen. One evening while peeling an onion for vegetarian chilli, he had a *eureka* moment. The onion was like a pebble tossed into the pool of his own mind. The ripples spread. *Maybe a man is like an onion,* he thought. *Perhaps if I peel away everything that makes me, I'll find a core, a basic centre that defines me as male. That's where the difference has to be. The layers are the same for both sexes. As there is clearly a difference, and the difference is not in the layers, then it has to be at the core. It must be profound and unique.* He stirred the chilli in excitement. "That's where the essence of maleness is," he shouted at the onion. "At the centre of my being, when I strip away the layers. No wonder I haven't gotten anywhere. I've been looking outside myself. I should be riding a horse, when I'm looking for a horse."

∽ ↝

Howcum developed a research program. He decided to get rid of everything about himself that was ephemeral and illusory. Like a sculptor reveals an image by chiselling away pieces of stone, he would shed the parts that hid Howcum Harold.

When he was ready, he took a sabbatical from his post at the university and returned to Tuckahoe to remove himself from the influences of everyday life. His program was rigorous. He knew the price of insight was suffering. He meditated, fasted, performed acts of penance, engaged in self-flagellation, and undertook hard physical trials that left him exhausted and near collapse. He became detached, lost weight and colour disappeared from his features. His eyes burned and he developed the far away look of a madman.

Folks became worried. They rarely saw him, and when they did he spoke to no one. After spotting him rolling nude in the snow late one night, Lydia Mergenfelter commented, "He's either drunk, gone insane or turned Catholic." Lydia was a sober, well-adjusted Lutheran.

One by one, he put away the things of this world. Pride, anger, boastfulness, ambition and material desires fell. Eventually he shed his past. Without a history, there is no ego and one day, barely conscious and weak from hunger, he felt the last shred of it slip away.

Exhausted, he contemplated what no one had ever seen — his naked centre, his core, his essence — the absolute transcendental pure state of a man revealed — his inner nature exposed in all its splendour. He trembled at the sudden clarity of the answer. Howcum Harold was horny.

❧ ❧

The exertion had taken its toll and Howcum's health was fragile. It deteriorated and he died shortly after his discovery. The results of his research were never published.

Lydia Mergenfelter spoke to Reverend Davies after Howcum's funeral. "It's a shame," she said. "He had all the talent in the world. He could have had everything — a wife, a nice home, a family. He might have become an electrician or even a master welder. He threw it all away. Sometimes I wonder what makes people like him tick."

PROUD NOT FEED CHICKENS

Folks who know about these things say it was bound to happen. Once Olga Faye Semenoff set her sights on Christopher Mitchell, God Herself couldn't have changed the direction of Christopher's fate. They say that when his horse was led to water, it sucked it up like a dehydrated sponge.

Olga Faye was the oldest of six girls in a family piloted by her mother, Big Fannie Semenoff. Fannie had been alone since her husband, Anton, died in a tragic accident shortly after Verna Faye, the youngest, was born. Anton was crushed to death when he accidentally got himself between Ferd, a two thousand pound Hereford bull, and a young heifer with whom Ferd was hoping to become carnally involved.

Providing for Olga Fay and her sisters was daunting, but Fannie was equal to the challenge. Her work ethic was unmatched. Neighbours complained about the number of hours she drove her tractor before allowing silence to settle on the late-night landscape. Seeding, haying and harvesting came naturally to her and she proved as capable as any man. She had a keen eye for livestock and Semenoff steers commanded premium prices at the local auction.

She also took on the operation of Anton's still. Under her careful administration quality improved, and soon a steady stream of customers were making regular treks to the Semenoff farm. The still was distant from the house, so the finished product was wrapped in blankets and hidden in the woodpile until sold. Things went well and the family prospered.

Olga Faye was sixteen at the time of her father's death. She was a slim, active girl with undistinguished looks. Only her eyes were different. They sparkled with possibility, unlike the opaque heaviness through which her sisters viewed the world.

She had an intense love of birds and animals and spent hours hiking the prairie, learning the habits of all who dwelt there. She also made friends with the farm animals, and was on particularly good terms with a pony named Stephanie and with Ferd, the huge bull that had crushed her father. She visited them daily, bringing a sprinkle of sugar for Stephanie and a handful of barley chop for Ferd. Both recognised her and came running when she approached.

Olga Faye was also blessed with a lively intelligence and a stubborn optimism that shone through her plainness. By the time she was seventeen, she knew what she wanted from life.

"She's a go-getter," Mr. Armshank, the school principal, told Fannie. "You should be proud."

"Sure I proud," Fannie answered. "But proud not feed chickens or milk cows."

While not particularly religious, Fannie was driven by a spiritual zeal that was anchored firmly in pragmatism. She taught Olga Faye and the other girls the mysteries of the world. Under her tutelage, they learned what they needed to know. Academics were left to Mr. Armshank and the school. Fannie's lessons were practical and important — proper deportment in a society awash in loose morals, and how to recognise decent candidates in the alcoholic flotsam that served as Tuckahoe's pool of potential husbands.

A whirlwind of protective energy, Fannie was clear and explicit. As each girl squeezed into adolescence, her mother took her aside. "You got treasure there, you don't give away," she said, waving in the general direction of the girl's treasure. "You keep it. It's for making babies, not for making fun. You want fun, you pick berries, can peas, make borscht."

"But Mama, that's work, not fun," Polly Faye complained.

"It's more fun than changing diapers," Fannie told her. "So when boy drives you home, keep car door open and knees closed . . . always, until you find man to keep. He should be strong and not so smart. He only needs enough *oomph* in his head, so he can feed kids that come from oomph in his pants. It only takes once to make baby. More is waste of husband's energy — he could be working. But sometimes okay to have fun. Remember, hard-up man like bull. He not care which heifer in pasture."

The lessons stuck. Two of the girls found local boys with the right amount of oomph in both places. They married and started families. But not Olga Faye. She had higher aspirations.

For as long as she could remember she'd been ambitious, although not in the manner of other girls. She desired neither money, prestige nor movie-star looks. She did not crave the security of a home. Hers was an ambition of a different sort — an ambition of the heart.

She wished for a special man: a man who was honest, intelligent, and sensitive; a man who would understand her need to do things other than butcher chickens and can beets; a man who could listen and sympathise; a man comfortable in places other than Louie's Cafe; a man whose social circle extended beyond the Cenotaph Hotel Beer Parlour. All this she dreamed, never able to articulate, even to herself, how she would go about finding such a man — or even if such a man existed.

Fannie was swept away by Olga Faye's ambition. It far surpassed her own. As a girl, it had never occurred to her to question her role, station, prospects or future. She found Olga

Faye's presumption breathtaking. Moreover, it nurtured a hope she'd secretly harboured for years — that at least one of her daughters might be made for better things than life in Tuckahoe.

Olga Faye's dilemma also perplexed her. "Where will you find this superman who will leap grain elevators in one jump?" she asked.

Olga Faye had no answer, but she refused to let a lack of possibility or the passage of years dampen her enthusiasm. By the time she was twenty-one, she and Fannie were the only ones not convinced that she was destined to be an old maid, soon to be as useful as Christmas cake in January. Thus, when the Tuckahoe School Board employed a young Englishman named Christopher Mitchell, both mother and daughter sensed the opportunity of a lifetime.

The bankruptcy of his father's estate had forced Christopher to seek under-employment in the far-off prairie west. He was near the end of his resources when offered the teaching position. He jumped at it. In this remote locale, lack of funds was not a social impediment.

Christopher came on the morning train. By noon, word of his arrival had spread to all the ladies who had no ticket in the local marriage raffle. Rumours proliferated, but there was only one basic fact: an unmarried male was staying at Tooperman's Boarding House. By mid-afternoon, the Toopermans had been visited by most of the town's single females. They all hoped to catch a glimpse of the biggest thing to hit Tuckahoe since the hailstorm of '49.

An exception was Olga Faye. She'd spotted Christopher at the train station and her heart had fluttered. *This man was worth the wait*, she thought.

And she was right. Christopher was everything Olga Faye dreamed, and more. He was the only scion of an upper class family that had fallen on hard financial times. He had manners, education and confidence. To top it off, God had seen fit to give him a gentle and unassuming disposition.

While his peers wallowed in their position in the social hierarchy, he pursued the works of Shelley, Wordsworth and Keats. He had a poet's soul and spent long hours composing idylls to a love left on England's distant shore. Little did he know that after he boarded ship, his far-away sweetheart set about boarding his best friend.

The first order of business was to invite Christopher to dinner — a dinner Fannie intended to cook. However, Christopher suspected the motivation behind the calls he was getting from the town's unmarried women. True to his distant love, he declined them all.

Fannie was in no hurry. She knew Mrs. Tooperman's reputation as a cook. "We wait," she told Olga Faye. "Hungry man is like seagull. He eat anywhere."

Fannie was right about Mrs. Tooperman's bad culinary habits. The timing of her phone call was impeccable: just as Christopher was served a plate of roast chicken complete with feathers. He accepted the invitation and headed to the bathroom.

Fannie was ecstatic. "I will cook and you say you did," she said to Olga Faye. "I will also get bottle of dandelion wine."

But Olga Faye was stubborn. "I'll do the cooking," she said. "I'm not going to pretend. But I will serve the wine."

The evening was a disaster. Olga Faye's ambition had never extended to the kitchen, and Christopher turned out to be a teetotaller. Fannie realised the route to his heart was not going to be through Olga Faye's cooking. She looked at the untouched bottle of wine. "A man who don't drink is good for husband, but no good for possible husband," she said. "We need plan. We should find out what he's interested in."

Determining Christopher's interests proved easy. Mary Faye was in his class at school. "All he talks about is birds and animals," she said. "He goes hiking every weekend with some girls named Flora and Fauna . . . and he likes poems."

Fannie was disappointed. "How are we going to get him interested in you, Olga Faye? He's sissy — only interested in birds and words. Maybe he's no good after all."

Olga Faye was fed up. "That's enough, Mama. I don't want your help anymore. I can find my own man."

Fannie was well aware of Olga Faye's stubborn streak. *We missed best opportunity,* she thought. *Now she is old maid, too fussy to ever find man.*

But Olga Faye was just getting started. The next day she paid a visit to the school after class. "Hello, Mr. Mitchell," she said. "I hear you're interested in birds. Have you ever seen a *Saskatchewan slough pump*?"

"A what?"

"A Saskatchewan slough pump. It's a big brown bird that lives in the marsh on our farm. It makes a noise like a pump."

"No, I haven't seen one. It must be rare. Did you say they live on your farm?"

"Yes. There's lots of them. I'd be happy to show you. They're easier to see when it's getting dark. Come over tomorrow evening."

"I'd be delighted. I don't know the fauna of this marvellous country. I appreciate a guide who can introduce me."

Olga Faye made a face. *He didn't mention Flora,* she thought. *But if Mary Faye's right, he already knows Fauna. If he thinks I'm going to introduce him to her, he's swimming in the wrong slough.*

She spent the next day boning up on the poetry Mary Faye was studying at school. She was excited and found it difficult to concentrate on her kid sister's textbook.

Christopher arrived in late afternoon, and by dusk they were slogging through a marsh west of the Semenoff yard, looking for the rare bird. Soft, sticky mud clutched his shoes. He stumbled and grabbed Olga Faye's hand. She gripped him tightly and didn't let go, pulling him to a stop. "Listen," she said.

A cool evening breeze carried the unmistakable sound of a pump over the waving marsh grass — *oonck-a-tsoonck . . . oonck-a-tsoonck . . . oonck-a-tsoonck.*

"What is it?" asked Christopher.

"That's the slough pump. We should be able to see it."

Cautiously, she moved her head around. "There," she whispered.

"Where? I don't see anything."

Olga Faye moved behind him and put her hands on his cheeks. Slowly she rotated his head. "There," she said again.

And there it was — narrow head, beak pointed straight up, long spotted brown neck stretched out, pretending to be a blade of marsh grass.

Christopher was disappointed. "I've seen that in a book," he said. "It's an American bittern."

He's not so smart, she thought to herself. *Everybody knows a slough pump when they see one.* They continued. Mutual excitement started to build as they spotted red-winged blackbirds, Canada geese, trumpeter swans, even a prairie chicken — crouched, hiding from their noise. A coyote picked up their scent and shadowed them. When Olga Faye pointed him out, Christopher said, "Wolf!" and shivered. He moved closer to her.

He's afraid of a coyote, she thought. *That's cute.*

It was almost dark by the time they started back. They held the barbed wire for each other and crawled through into the Semenoff yard. Halfway to the house, Christopher was startled by snorting and the sound of wild pounding hooves. He jumped and grabbed Olga Faye's shoulder.

"It's the bull," she shouted. "Quick, follow me." She took his arm and dragged him up the woodpile. They clambered to the top and Christopher looked back. He swallowed and fear fell over him like hail on a bumper crop. A gigantic bull had started up the woodpile behind them. Its front legs reached to just below where they stood. It snorted and waved its massive head from side to side like a medieval dragon. Deadly horns pointed straight at them, framing wild eyes.

"Can he climb?" Christopher breathed.

"No," she said. "But we'll have to stay here until he goes."

He shivered. The moon was up and the night air chilly. The bull backed down off the woodpile. In the moonlight he could see it snuffling and pacing a few feet from the bottom.

"It's cold," he said, hugging himself to keep warm.

Olga Faye knelt, scattered some blocks and in seconds excavated a depression in the top of the woodpile. Then she scrambled halfway down the side opposite the bull. She scattered more blocks and retrieved two blankets and a bottle of homebrew. She lined the hollow with one blanket. Then she lay down, covered herself with the other and held up one corner. Christopher hesitated and then joined her. He lay stiff with his arms at his sides as the cold gradually penetrated the blanket.

"We'll have to huddle to keep warm," Olga Faye said.

"Yes, I suppose so, but only to keep from freezing," Christopher answered.

Olga Faye took the cap off the bottle.

"What is it?" he asked.

"Have some," she said. "It'll warm your insides. It's my mother's medicine, made especially for cold nights."

Christopher sniffed the open bottle. "It's alcohol," he said. "You know I don't drink."

"Go ahead," Olga Faye whispered as she snuggled against him. "It really will keep you warm."

"I suppose it's permissible in an emergency," he said.

He sipped from the bottle. The liquid burned its way to his stomach. He lay back on the blanket, enjoying the sensation. The sky was bright with twinkling autumn stars and he felt the warmth of Olga Faye's body pressed against him. She sighed comfortably and moved closer.

Far above them a lone mosquito hawk shrieked as it hunted dinner. "Hail to thee, blithe spirit," Olga Faye said.

Christopher grinned. "I think they're all blithe spirits," he said. "But I shouldn't be here with you. I have a lady friend in England."

Olga Faye held her breath. "Is she coming to Tuckahoe?" she asked.

"No," Christopher answered. "She refuses to leave home."

Olga Faye relaxed. What was it her mother had said? "A hungry man sleeps in any pasture . . . " or something like that.

"Are you hungry?" she asked.

"Why ever do you ask?" Christopher said. "But, now that you've brought it up, the answer is yes. I'm ravenous."

Olga Fay smiled. *Sometimes Mama's very smart,* she thought. She took a drink and passed the bottle to Christopher. This time he didn't hesitate. He lifted his arm, placed it under her shoulders and squeezed her to him. She complied, melding her body with his. Slow and tentative, they began to explore each other. The intimacy stunned and delighted them both.

As day broke they stirred, each reluctant to break the spell that bound them to the wooden nest and to each other. Finally, Christopher raised himself on one arm. The bull was still watching, standing at the bottom of the woodpile.

Olga Faye stood up. "I'll distract him. You go down the other side and run for the house," she said.

Without waiting for an argument, she started toward the bull. Christopher watched for a moment, then scrambled down the far side and ran.

Olga Faye glanced back. Christopher's heels were turning up so fast he seemed to be kneeling in prayer. She smiled, jumped to the bottom of the woodpile and pulled a bag from her jacket pocket.

"Here Ferd, here's your chop. You did a great job. You could be an actor." She held out the bag and playfully scratched between his eyes as he nuzzled for the long-denied treat.

She left it for him, climbed back over the woodpile and ran for the house. Christopher, watching from the safety of the porch, said out loud, "My God, she's brave. I've never seen anyone like her."

"Yes, she is," Big Fannie said, coming up behind him. "And she's smart, too."

LOVE, POETRY *and* SEAGULLS

It was five o'clock on a Saturday afternoon and Henry Wadsworth Douziak had stopped his tractor in the middle of an eighty acre field. He was staring at some seagulls, those white birds that soar gracefully in the sky but are awkward when they land. He was staring at the seagulls but he wasn't thinking about them.

Henry was thinking of love. More specifically, he was thinking he would like to be in love. Deep within himself he was afraid, though not of love, or of being in love. He was afraid of *not* being in love, at least of not being in the kind of love he imagined love should be. From the time he had discovered poetry, Henry had developed a model against which he measured all feelings and emotions. He knew that love should be chaste and pure, as unsullied as a newborn's morality:

Where thoughts serenely sweet express
How pure, how dear their dwelling place.

. . .

A mind at peace with all below,
A heart whose love is innocent!

It was Henry's destiny that evening to attend the wedding dance of his cousin Freda in the neighbouring town of Stoneboat Creek. It was also his destiny to gaze for a moment into the clear eyes of Sylvia Ann Slipnicker, the brilliant daughter of Adele and Mervin Slipnicker. She was a girl who lived inside her head, and the only truly intoxicating moments in her life had occurred there. Behind Sylvia's eyes he would glimpse a kindred spirit and a promise.

Henry was short, five foot six, and folks in Tuckahoe described him as chunky. He had a stook of red hair that stood straight up and waved in the breeze like a nervous campfire. His complexion was a reflection of his hair. He was fidgety most of the time, given to confusion, sometimes inarticulate and he gave folks the impression of standing just behind himself. His friend Ernie said that when girls were around Henry acted like a puppy caught peeing on the carpet.

Apart from memorizing a few poems in English classes, Henry had shown no interest in school. He quit early and went to work on his father's farm. He was nineteen and had never had a girlfriend. Girls were not attracted to him and this caused a rust spot on his ego. So he hovered between his vision and reality — a poet's soul trapped in the body of a puppy.

How long he'd been sitting on the tractor, Henry didn't know. Certainly it was long enough; the seagulls had become impatient. A few raucous ones flew perilously close to his head to encourage him to continue turning up their dinner.

But Henry was too busy to drive. He was picturing love. You see, he had imagination. It wasn't the kind of imagination that ran free and created new ways of looking at the world. His was controlled and ranged only to the end of a leash he'd woven from twisted strands of poems. Though the level on his testosterone gauge read "Full", Henry's background had not given him enough raw material to manufacture truly erotic imagery. Thus, his experience was woefully inadequate for anything but the most cursory relationship with the opposite sex.

His love of poetry was a secret he now kept from the world. He had a passion for it all, but the verses of love were what captured him. He hoped that someday a girl would see the romantic soul that dwelt behind his physical imperfections:

And this maiden she lived with no other thought
Than to love and be loved by me.

❧ ❧

His name was really Harold. He'd been christened Henry Wadsworth because of two incidents that occurred when he was ten years old. He'd accompanied his mother to the hen house to gather eggs but a fox had got there first. The nests were empty and few hens were alive. His mother related the tale to his father at dinner. Harold, mouth full of perogies, pushed back from the table and mumbled,

"For Time shall teach thee soon the truth,
There are no birds in last year's nest!"

A few weeks later, Tuckahoe was hit by a summer storm. Mr. Douziak's heart sank as he surveyed newly cut hay becoming mouldy in the field. Later that week, he made the mistake of mentioning the hay to Baldy Potter.

Baldy usually spent long days exercising his tongue in front of Louie's Café. It was said that if Tuckahoe's social scale were to be measured in Fahrenheit, Baldy would register forty below zero. He took delight in the hardships facing anyone with a purpose in life and chortled as he commiserated with Mr. Douziak about the hay. "It's God's way of making things even for the bumper crop you had two years ago," he said.

Christopher Mitchell, a new teacher in Tuckahoe, overheard Baldy's statement. "That's not true," he said. "God doesn't go around evening things out."

"Oh yes, He does," piped up young Harold, who was studying his reflection in the café window.

"Into each life some rain must fall,
Some days must be dark and dreary."

"Why, that's Longfellow," Christopher said. "Where did you learn it?"

Harold continued to stare at the window.

"I'll be," Christopher said. "The boy's quoting Henry Wadsworth Longfellow. He must have been reading in the school library."

"He does it at home, too," Mr. Douziak said, and told them about the fox in the henhouse.

"Henry Wadsworth Douziak," Baldy mused and smirked. "Just think, Tuckahoe's own 'poet lariat'. I guess we've lassoed us some fame now."

Harold, or "Henry" as he came to be known, made a face at himself in Louie's window.

🐦 🐦

At the wedding, Henry looked forward to an evening of crowded solitude at the back of the dance hall. He liked to watch the girls dancing, their legs flashing under crinolines as they twirled through the two-step. They were held intimately by sweaty-faced young men: men who lived in the moment and who spoke rudely to him as they shoved by to dance with visions in make-up — visions who batted eyes and uncrossed legs in damp anticipation.

Henry was startled when, through the crowd, he saw a girl as pretty and enticing as a golden daffodil. She was keeping the wall warm with her back and peering at him with shining grey eyes. When she saw him looking, her face turned the colour of a prairie sunset and she moved her gaze to a spot above Henry's head. Mesmerized, he walked toward her, Wordsworth's lines flowing from his lips:

"A violet by a mossy stone
Half hidden from the eye!

Fair as a star, when only one
Is shining in the sky."

She shivered when she realized he was directing the words at her. Then she smiled. "That's beautiful," she said, blushing again. "Verse is a door through which a poet can enter your soul and stir emotion."

Henry had never heard anything like it. Her voice was like ecstasy sung by a nightingale. "Yes, yes," he breathed, "and if the poet stirs the same emotion in two people, he creates a link between them."

Sylvia Ann was tall, with wild black hair. She was dressed carelessly in a long yellow gown that failed to disguise the generous proportions of the length of her. She was also attired in an intelligence that far eclipsed local norms, and from the time she'd been a child her teachers had recognized the genius behind her quiet demeanour. Now twenty, she had already completed a degree in literature and was taking a well-earned rest before leaving to pursue graduate studies in England.

She hoped a year off would take away a feeling of unease that appeared at unexpected times. It was a vague feeling that something was missing, a strange intuition that Elizabethan poetry provided only a slice of what she needed to know in life. Her studies had left no time for dating so, like Henry, her only experience in the realm of love had occurred in her fantasies. She suffered from a terrible shyness, and apart from her professors Henry was the first male to whom she had ever spoken without her tongue collapsing around its words.

His breath was whisked away so that no other verse came to his lips. He became drenched in sweat. Unfamiliar emotions flooded through him the way wild water overwhelms a river bank. *She's wonderful,* he thought.

A crowd of people moved between them and she was gone. But the wall had been breached. Henry was absolutely, utterly and forever smitten.

An idea skittered around his brain like a billiard ball on a pool table. It caromed off his feelings and dropped into the corner pocket of his consciousness: *maybe there's hope,* he thought. *Maybe there's someone for me.*

The seed planted that night sprouted into longing, a longing that grew and blossomed into fantasy. But he was afraid. What if he never saw her again? What if she wanted nothing to do with him? He was frightened and attracted at the same time. Something in her eyes had caught him. He felt like a hooked fish slowly and inexorably being pulled toward a boat.

Weeks went by. Unused to being smitten, everything reminded him of her and he became obsessed. She materialized in his mind as he pounded fence posts; she was with him as he milked cows; her presence was in each rock he picked. There was no solace even in poetry. Every verse evoked the image of her untamed hair, carefree dress and ample body:

A sweet disorder in the dress
Kindles in clothes a wantonness:

. . .

Do more bewitch me than when art
Is too precise in every part

Shaken and confused, he resolved to forget her. He took long walks alone. He drove miles in his father's pickup. He worked every daylight hour and played solitaire in the evening. He even recited limericks, and sometimes, in the busyness of the day, he was able to force her from his mind.

But she returned in his dreams. He drank gallons of coffee to stay awake but it made him sick, an abdominal manifestation of the ache in his heart.

His friend Ernie was sympathetic. "I once felt like you," he said. "I couldn't get my mind off a certain girl."

"What did you do?" asked Henry. "Did you ask her out?"

"Yes, I did. But she wouldn't go. It made everything worse. I fantasized about her all the time. Every night, I dreamed I was making love to her. I almost went crazy."

"Did you eventually get together?"

"Well . . . sort of," said Ernie.

"What do you mean . . . sort of?"

"Put it this way," said Ernie. "We made love but she wasn't there."

"You mean . . . "

"Yep. I Goddam near wore it off before I got over her." He sniggered. "It might be your only solution, so to speak."

Harold turned away. "Thanks, Ernie. You're a big help," he said.

Big help or not, time plus a sprinkle or two of Ernie's advice worked magic. Henry began to feel the beauty of unrequited love, of pure yearning with no hope.

Then, one crisp fall Sunday, he saw her walking in Tuckahoe. His resolve evaporated, and without a thought he followed. She went into the Anglican Church. Henry quietly sat down behind her.

Sylvia Ann wasn't the least bit religious but believed she ought to be. She had been increasingly on edge since the wedding dance and she couldn't get Henry's crimson face out of her mind. She explained everything to her dog, Percy Bysshe. "I don't understand," she said. "I feel nervous all the time. I think it's because I have no foundation. My life is empty."

She embarked on a mission to discover her own spirituality and felt the place to start was in church. It was only by chance that Henry saw her at the beginning of her quest, when she had not yet had time to mistake dogma for insight, or emotions for religious experience.

An intense girl, Sylvia Ann knew she was intelligent but didn't know what that might mean in the world of relationships. She was passionate for the written word and felt that poetry could express the longing in her soul. *What* she longed for she hadn't yet defined. Again, she confided to Percy Bysshe, "Sometimes, in the morning, just as I'm waking up, it's almost painful . . . the ache I mean. I feel flat . . . like a tire . . . like I need to be inflated, only I don't have a pump."

It was Sylvia Ann's intention to stay away from emotional entanglements. She knew a relationship might hinder her plans to attend graduate school. Not fully aware of the nature of her feelings, she beefed up her resolve by reciting a prayer:

"Pan, grant that I may never prove
So great a slave to fall in love,"

She was surprised when she saw Henry in the pew behind her — the fiery-haired man who had made her heart quiver at the dance. Her knees and her resolve weakened when he whispered to her outside the church. "Would you like a Coke at Louie's?"

"Uh . . . uh . . . oh, yes," she breathed, stepping back to preserve her balance and her decorum.

At first the meeting was clumsy, filled with silence and punctuated by simultaneous conversation as each tried to escape an awkwardness that threatened to undermine everything. Henry was convinced she saw him as a witless fool. She felt like an idiot and began to die inside.

But such is the chemistry of longing and the power of hormones to obscure the senses: there was no danger of one eyeing the other in a poor light. So the first contact, while not a raging success, was not a disaster either, and both came away quite sure they would see each other again.

And they did. They met for coffee and for walks along the river, and once the ice was broken, they talked. Lord, how they talked. A tide of words surged from Henry's heart, jammed briefly in his throat and then took flight the way frightened ducks burst out of a quiet slough. Breathlessly she replied, unaware of what she said. They discussed the weather, literature, world affairs, people they knew, local politics and their families. But most of all they discussed poetry. It drew them together, fused their hearts and provided each a glimpse into the other's soul.

One thing they never discussed was their own feelings. What was developing was fragile and it was too soon to bring it into the open. Instinctively, each knew the bonds being formed needed time to strengthen. To stir a romantic soup too early can make a hash of everything.

This was remarkable, considering that both felt they were participating in a miracle — much like a mother when she first takes her newborn in her arms. The feeling was awe, not of each other but of the love they were creating, a love composed of equal parts tenderness, concern, admiration, wonder, curiosity, camaraderie and, yes, desire. Through the winter of their mutual obsession they discussed a thousand things, though neither remembered even a tenth of what they talked about.

Another thing that wasn't discussed was Sylvia Ann's plan to go to England. Intent on their immediate journey, neither cared to consider bumps that might appear down the road.

One spring day, seated on the river bank, staring at glistening spots of sun-dappled water and watching a beaver slowly make its way upstream camouflaged by a branch of poplar leaves, Sylvia Ann, as if in a trance, recited:

"Glory be to God for dappled things—
For skies of couple-colour as a brinded cow;
For rose-moles all in stipple upon trout that swim;"

"Huh," said Henry, who had been pretending he was on Westminster Bridge.

Suddenly she could stand it no longer. She turned away but the spots of light stayed in front of her eyes, giving the impression the world was a shiftless place that didn't change no matter where you looked.

"Henry," she said. "I guess we've discussed everything there is to discuss."

He looked at her. "I guess we have," he said.

"Except one thing," she replied. "We've never talked about what we think or feel about each other." Her voice caught and her knees trembled.

"I guess not." He picked a piece of marsh grass and tore it into small pieces.

"Maybe some things are better left unsaid." She plucked imaginary lint from her sweater.

Henry tore the small pieces into smaller pieces. "Maybe talking about some things would spoil everything," he said.

"Maybe," she said, her voice dull. The sun fell behind the willows, leaving his face in shadow. She looked at the river again, but the water was grey and the beaver had disappeared.

"Let's head back," he said.

He drove slowly, carefully, until he was parked behind the Slipnicker house. They sat silent for a few minutes. "Maybe we could, just a little," he said.

Her heart jumped. "Could what?" she asked.

TUCKAHOE SLIDEBOTTLE

"You know," he said, "talk about our feelings — what we think about each other."

Sylvia Ann decided not to let him off easy. "You first," she said.

"Oh, no. You brought it up. You start."

"Oh, Henry," she sighed. "Let's start together. You know I've cared for you from the first time I saw you."

Though it was what he hoped to hear, the temperature of Henry's feet dropped ten degrees. It wasn't the fear of something never happening. This was the fear of change, of the abandonment of something he was used to. For all his longing, the male flight gene was alive and idling in Henry.

Sylvia Ann was also uneasy. It was a big step. A declaration of feelings could never be undone. No matter what changed in the future, how she felt for this man here and now was about to be put on display for him to see. Trepidation swept over her and her breath caught in her throat. She gulped at the evening air and plunged ahead. "Yes, from the first time I saw you, I've thought of no one else."

"Me too," he said.

She waited for more but he was silent. *He might as well have said "ditto"*, she thought.

Finally he spoke. "From the first time, me too," he said.

Again silence. "Yes, me too," he repeated.

"What?" She was confused.

"I've had feelings for you from the start. I think of you all the time. I can't sleep and I can't work."

"Oh," she said.

"Is that all?" he asked.

"No, I'm like that, too."

They left the truck and he walked her to the door. Percy Bysshe watched Henry with suspicion from the edge of the

Slipnicker veranda. He growled and barked. Henry jumped and then, in a flash of inspiration, took her hands in his.

"Sylvia, thy beauty is to me
Like those Nicéan barks of yore,"

he said, eyeing Percy Bysshe over the top of Sylvia Ann's head.

They didn't kiss, although both anticipated it. Kissing would have been an admission of passion, a blemish on the pure love each imagined. Instead of passion, they became serious. They stared longer into each other's eyes. They quit talking and sighed a lot.

✺ ✺

The first kiss was an accident. They had taken to going for twilight walks along the shore of Blackjacket Lake and had stopped to look at a path of moonlight across the water. A loon was swimming in the path and filling the evening with its lonely call. She turned to him and he to her.

"The gray sea, and the long black land;
And the yellow half-moon large and low;"

he said.

"And a voice less loud, through its joys and fears,
Than the two hearts beating each to each!"

she replied.

Their breath mingled and they stared into each other's eyes. She lowered her head and rested it on his shoulder. He nuzzled her hair. She raised her face and looked at him. His lips parted. She bent over and puckered. He came closer and shut his eyes. She inhaled a full breath, leaned forward and . . . missed!

For a moment she suckled on the end of his nose. He pecked at her chin. Flushed with embarrassment, she pulled away. He opened his eyes and closed them again. She looked at him and desire overcame embarrassment. Their lips connected and it happened. Time stopped and neither was willing to start it. The loon replayed his lonely dirge, the moon dipped into the lake and Henry's whole being became submerged in this woman.

"How do I love thee? Let me count the ways." he thought.

And, as if reading his mind, she whispered to his lips: *"I love thee to the depth and breadth and height/ My soul can reach."*

After this they took to kissing quite a lot. In fact, it's safe to say they did little else. Their tongues, previously employed in conversation, now worked overtime in silence. They experimented with every known form of the oscular art, and with some unknown ones too. Hours were spent with lips locked, hot breath coming and going loudly through their noses. From his slow start Henry became proficient, like a neophyte on skates may become a professional hockey player.

Each attended movies alone hoping to learn technique from the stars. Because the same film played in Tuckahoe a week after it showed in Stoneboat Creek, Henry was always behind. Sylvia Ann was surprised at how fast he caught on. He, in turn, wondered at her skills, skills he thought were secrets known only in Hollywood.

The surprise and wonder grew to uncertainty and then to mild irritation. When Henry had a flat tire on the pick-up and arrived late, she lectured him. "I know you had a flat," she said. "But if you left enough time for contingencies you wouldn't be late."

"Excuse me," he said. "I didn't know you could be late for walks in the moonlight. I guess the moon doesn't come up if we're not there by a certain time."

Soon confusion joined irritation. *Why?* She asked herself:
Doat on his Imperfections, though I spy
Nothing to Love; I Love and know not why.

This state of affairs was not precipitated by kissing knowledge or a lack thereof. Nor was being late the cause. The real culprits were the constant frustration of increasing desire, the attendant guilt and unspoken passion, none of which fit into a model of pure and chaste love. Indeed, if their fluctuating hormone levels could have been harnessed like the rise and fall of tides, Henry and Sylvia would have generated enough power to light a small city.

Again Henry confided to Ernie, "I don't understand it. One minute we're nuts about each other and the next we're pecking away like cannibal chickens. I can't stand it. I love her but she drives me crazy."

"You're classic," said Ernie. "Both of you need to get laid." He spoke with the authority of someone who has spent years eavesdropping on conversations around a pool table.

"Stop it," said Henry sharply. "She's not that kind of girl and we don't love each other that way."

"Oh, she's not and you don't, eh?" Ernie raised his eyebrows in disbelief. "Then why are you spending every waking moment necking? You're pouring gas on a campfire. It's going to blaze out of control and you're both going to get burnt." Ernie didn't know poetry but if he had, he might have said,

Gather ye rosebuds while ye may,
Old Time is still a-flying;
And this same flower that smiles to-day,
To-morrow will be dying.

Although Henry didn't admit it, he and Sylvia Ann had already come close to gathering rosebuds. Lying in the grass at Blackjacket Lake, only a fortuitous cloudburst had kept their virtue intact. The episode frightened him.

For her part, Sylvia Ann had decided she wanted more. Her resolve to remain unentangled was history. She didn't know how to communicate her need to Henry and she was too bashful to take the initiative. The twin obstacles of modesty and her inability to declare her desire seemed insurmountable. She was also torn between the lure of graduate school and her longing for Henry. The pressure of diminishing time brought her close to despair.

Unwittingly, Henry came to the rescue by reading Emily Dickinson to her one evening.

"Rowing in Eden—
Ah, the sea!
Might I moor, tonight,
In thee!"

He stopped, shocked at what he'd just read.

"Of course, Henry," she said without thinking . . . and like that, it happened! The dam burst. Passion washed over them. They took their first swim in carnal waters. They looked at that world from the inside — and it was unreal, a place of magic — Wonderland, Never-Never Land and the Big Rock Candy Mountain all rolled into one.

Later they thought there might be a moral benefit in trying to curtail their sexual activity. The resolve lasted less than an hour, so they decided to try rationalization instead.

"We're old enough," said Henry.

"We love each other," said Sylvia Ann.

"Our love transcends right and wrong," said Henry.

"It doesn't matter what others think," said Sylvia Ann.

"We're alone in the world," said Henry

And indeed, it did seem as if only they existed. The intensity of their desire set them apart. Every day, the resolve to be resolved melted away as quickly as buttons, zippers, hooks, ties and laces could be undone. They laughed at the beauty of their feelings and yelled in delirious joy.

"I love you, Henry," she said.

"I love and idolize you," he said, more loudly.

"I love, idolize and cherish you!" she shouted.

He rolled down the window of the pickup. "I love, idolize, cherish and adore Sylvia Ann!" he bellowed to the town.

They made up spicy games and savoured every taste. "How much do you love me, Henry?" she asked.

"As fair art thou, my bonie lass,
So deep in luve am I;
And I will luve thee still, my Dear,
Till a' the seas gang dry,"

he answered. "And how much do you love me, Sylvia Ann?"
Playfully, she replied,

"Till a' the seas gang dry, my Dear,
And the rocks melt wi' the sun;
I will luve thee still my Dear,
While the sands o' life shall run."

They became intemperate and made love everywhere and anytime: morning in the pickup, under the stars, in her parents' bedroom at noon, in the middle of the eighty acre field, even the back booth in Louie's Café! Every time was the first and the magic didn't fade.

Sometimes they lay still — she rhythmically squeezing and he deep inside, swelling in response, staring at each other, pressure building, until . . . unable to stand it, one of them would thrust, a signal for their naked hips to strain together until, in an agony of passion they exploded and spun deliciously into that moment the French call *la petite mort*. Then, as close to tasting the soul of another as it's possible to come, they plashed gently back to reality in each other's wet softness.

She felt herself shameless and revelled in her power to control his pleasure. He shivered at the sight of her naked and spent hours finding the right touch to coax her from one sensation to another. For both, the years of aloneness melted away. To say they took to sex the way a duck takes to water would be inadequate. It was more the way wetness takes to water. Sex became the defining property of their lives.

A baseball thrown into the sky arcs towards the sun, pauses at the zenith and then, in a mirror image of its rise, falls back to earth. Its own weight ensures the fall. Like a baseball, Henry and Sylvia Ann's wondrous allure for each other carried the weight of its own downfall. Henry was aware of Sylvia Ann's unspoken need to go to graduate school and she knew he knew. The mutual awareness cast a silent shadow across their delight.

For a time Henry felt himself the luckiest person in the world, then, like a poor man who becomes wealthy and dreads a return to poverty, anxiety took root in him. "I don't think I could stand it if you weren't here," he told her. " . . . if you didn't love me."

"But I'll always love you," she said. "I'm addicted to you. I can't exist without you."

"I'm the addict — a Sylviaholic," he replied and squeezed her to him, but the foreboding stayed in his belly.

The pressure on Sylvia Ann carried its own toxin. *Is it me?* she wondered. *Or is it just the sex he wants?* The worry gnawed in her belly and took up permanent residence. Every evening she waited at the window, petrified he wouldn't come. By the time she saw the dust rising from the road, a sick feeling had forced the joy from her body.

This state of affairs occasionally sparked a quarrel, but both realized arguing was only a mask for fear. To fight it they did things together: they went to dinner, they attended movies, they played scrabble and did crossword puzzles, but it wasn't entertainment and it wasn't medicine. It was emotional suicide. Their lovemaking became a kind of sexual *hara kiri* they used to slice away each other's niggling trepidation.

Afterwards, Henry would lie beside her in an agony of worry. Then, as if already abandoned, he shivered and twisted like a dying insect. Beside him, Sylvia Ann sweated uncertainty until the bed was damp:

My love is as a fever, longing still
For that which longer nurseth the disease;
Feeding on that which doth preserve the ill,
The uncertain sickly appetite to please.

Her psyche was delicate and she knew she couldn't bear it much longer. To immerse herself permanently in this man would be to founder in an ocean of anxiety. It wasn't a question of his love not being as strong as hers. It was the dread of losing her life, of giving up her potential, of not being all she could. There was only one way out. When fall approached, she spoke it out loud. "Henry, I have to leave soon, to go to England."

He shuddered. Fear curled round his stomach like eagle claws on a rabbit. He had known all along, of course, but had chosen not to think about it. "Let's get married," he said. "We can run away or we can live on the farm with my parents.

Come live with me and be my love,
And we will all the pleasures prove . . .

"I have to go," she said. "I can't live like this, always near panic and I don't know why. I'll be back. We can wait for each other. Maybe time will make everything okay."

"I could come with you," he pleaded.

"What would you do in England?" she asked.

And that said it all. It wasn't what he could do in England. The problem was what he couldn't do anywhere. He couldn't keep her. She had a world he wasn't part of. A mutual love of poetry wasn't enough. She was beyond him and would continue to grow. She already had. Inside both knew it, but they had continued to play the game as if they had a lifetime.

It came time for her to leave. They sat in the back booth in Louie's café. Sylvia Ann stirred her Coke with a straw. "I'm scared that I won't be able to live without you," she said.

"I'm terrified you'll forget me," Henry answered.

Then words failed them and they stared at each other across the table. After a while Sylvia Ann stood and walked out of the café. Henry felt lost, condemned to exist only in his mind and not in hers.

I am not yours, not lost in you,
Not lost, although I long to be
Lost as a candle lit at noon,
Lost as a snowflake in the sea.

Sylvia Ann became depressed and in the darkness of depression found the detachment to harden herself to the parting. After she left for England, the world became drab for Henry. Sometimes, drowsy after a restless sleep, he reached for her, but her absence penetrated his empty embrace and squeezed his heart until the pain drove him from his bed.

❧ ❧

It was late in the afternoon and Henry was alone. The seagulls were gone and the eighty acre field was cold and empty. Deep within himself Henry was still afraid, though not of the idea of love. He was afraid of the complications and the reality of love, elegant in dreams but awkward in practice. A fall breeze made him shiver. Sylvia Ann had been gone for a month. He couldn't imagine what would happen to him now.

The SMELLS *of* LONG AGO CATTLE

Usually I'm awake before she knocks. Tonight is no different. I hear the whisper of her hand on the wall as she makes her way along the dark hallway. Her fingers pat my door. Impatient, they start a frantic scratch that drives away sleep. She always comes to wake me when the wind howls and snow whips across the stubble; when white streaks strafe my window and ice pellets pop in rhythm on the glass.

The scratching stops. Her voice is intense, urgent. "Nathan, it's storming. You have to hold the light for your father."

Her robe rustles as she disappears down the hall. Now I have the responsibility. I lie there a moment, hypnotized by the unending snow on my window. Their life is troubled. She worries for my father but they no longer love each other.

🖋 🖋

Things were fine in the beginning. My earliest memory is them together. It was also the first time I felt fear. Mother was cooking. The door was open and I was playing where the sun warmed the linoleum. A shadow slithered across the floor, crawled up my legs and covered me. I was scared and couldn't breathe. After it passed, I looked up. A man was standing in the doorway. Sunlight framed his body and left his face hidden.

Mother stood by the stove. "Whatever you're selling, stranger, we don't need any," she said.

He came behind her and put his arms around her waist. "But I've got kisses like candy and rolls in the hay."

She laughed and turned. Her hands clasped his head and pulled him to her. "I'll take them all," she said.

They breathed each other for a long time before he pulled away. After he left, she sang and danced me around the room.

They met in the city where he'd gone for winter work. She was rescuing a cat from a tree. He'd grinned and climbed the tree.

Her life had been sheltered. He was wild as chain lightning. She said he had a laugh to light up a street. He said her eyes outshone the stars in a prairie sky. They courted intensely, in secret, then married quickly when she became pregnant.

Before my father, she'd never lived on a farm. Her life was books and music and friends. She traded them for crude men, diapers and loneliness. She was estranged from her family and no one came to visit, but for a while happiness cloaked their marriage like snow covers a vacant lot.

꿈 ꕥ

I bring my feet to the floor. There *is* urgency. If the storm is bad, he'll need the light to guide him home. I dress quickly, tiptoe out and pick up the lantern, filled and waiting in the kitchen.

Outside, it's cold. Snow blows into my eyes. The path is buried and my feet sink into the fresh drifts. I put my head down and move slow. Buildings are only memories in the swirling blizzard.

The wind pierces my jacket and frost stings my cheeks before I reach the barn. My fingers freeze to the metal latch. I rip them away and feel pain mixed with blood.

Inside, the barn is dark. Rats squeal in empty stalls and the smells of long-ago cattle fill my nostrils. I light the lantern and climb the stairs. The flickering light casts deformed shadows that dance and seem to shriek when the wind moans through the cracked walls.

The loft door creaks and driving snow threatens the flame. How will Father see the tiny light from far in the field? I hang the lantern in the small doorway and sit on an overturned bucket. Now there's nothing to do but watch and listen and keep the flame alive.

🖎 🖎

I don't remember when it started. One day she sang as she canned peas. Then resentment tinged her voice. It may have been my baby brothers. They're twins and they sapped her energy. They shackled her to the farm just when I started school. After they were born she moved from my father's bedroom and slept alone.

My brothers were sickly. She mothered them, hoed the garden and milked cows. Then she washed clothes. Father started to smell like beer and sleep late.

Sometimes he brought men home and demanded she cook for them. "How do, Louisa," he shouted as he clumped through the door, red eyes blinking and a ten-draft smile on his face. "I told the boys what a fine cook you are. How about whipping up a few steaks?"

He looked at Mother's face. "Or even some scrambled eggs," he whispered.

Mother slammed the frying pan on the stove. "You sold the last steer for beer money," she said. "You can damn well scramble your own eggs."

"Whatever, Louisa. The boys don't care. But you have to cook. You know I'm no good around a stove."

The two men behind Father sniggered and leered. "That's okay," Baldy Potter said. "We'll take a rain check on the steaks."

Mother always claimed that saying the right thing was like putting money in the bank — one earned good will instead of interest. Unfortunately, Baldy declared bankruptcy every time he opened his mouth. "I understand," he said. "Women who sleep alone often get testy."

He turned toward mother just as an egg smashed down onto his shiny head. "What did I say?" he complained, yolk dripping into his eyes. "Larry, she's a frustrated woman. You've got to control her before she kills someone."

Mother pulled a knife from a kitchen drawer.

"I've got to be going," Baldy shouted, already out the door. "I forgot. I told Bernie I'd meet him in Stoneboat Creek."

After a time Father stopped bringing his friends. He only came home himself, long after she'd dragged her tired body to bed. Occasionally he stayed away for days. I remember watching headlights move on my bedroom wall as he rounded the corner and came down the hill into our yard.

❧ ❧

I can't allow myself to get too much into memories. I might miss him when he spots the light and shouts. If I'm not paying full attention, the wind can grab his cry and whisk his words across the field so fast I'll never hear them. He always yells when he sees the lantern. I have to shout back and wave the light so he can follow it home.

The driving flakes are hypnotic. Tears freeze in my eyes. I feel like I could step out and walk across the field. Direction has no meaning. There is only me in the doorway and the snow reaching from outside. And there is him, out beyond where I can see his struggle. And there is the wait . . . always the wait, until he sees the lantern.

❧ ❧

Mother rarely left the farm. Sometimes, on a Sunday, she'd curl her hair, put on a dress and our neighbour, Mrs. Nelson, would take her to church. My father scoffed. "I know what the preacher wants, Louisa. It ain't your soul he's after. You're still a fine piece of woman, and that hellfire and brimstone bugger wants some."

"Don't be an idiot, Larry. Reverend Davies has no interest in me." She dismissed him as easy as she'd swat a fly at the kitchen table.

He clenched his fists, frustration puddling around him. "Louisa, I . . . I . . . ," he stammered.

But there was nothing to say. She swept into her room and locked the door. She enjoyed the freedom of leaving obligation on the other side of a bolted door. By inverting responsibility, she confined my father as securely as if she'd handcuffed him to the stove. He made burnt hamburgers and we all tiptoed when we passed her bedroom.

Once in a while, on a Saturday, we all went to town. Mother bundled up me and the twins, and Father drove. She shopped while he went for a cold one. Then we waited, sometimes for hours, outside the Cenotaph Hotel Beer Parlour. When Father came out, he blinked and shouted, "Louisa and the kids! I forgot you were here! What a pleasure!"

But it wasn't a pleasure. The ride home was erratic from loose gravel and looser accusations. Blame passed back and forth like a hockey puck. Then they stared straight ahead and glowered — the start of a thick silence that lasted days. In the back seat we rubbed frost from the window and took turns looking through the hole.

❧ ❧

The wind pauses, pitches forward and delivers a shout. I peer into the snow but can't see anything. I wave the lantern.

"Dad . . . Dad . . . over this way." A gust flings the words back in my face.

Then I see him staggering far out in the field. He waves and starts toward the barn. Then he's gone. The shadows play in the dark, covering and uncovering him. I keep waving the lantern and shouting.

When I glimpse him again, he's heading down the fence line toward the creek. It's the wrong way! He's turned the wrong way! I yell again. The wind howls, and I feel the silence he hears.

I wait, hoping he'll follow the fenceline back. But there's nothing. The wind rises from the snow and moves the clouds. The sky lightens. When I can see into the field, I look for his tracks. There's only fresh snow, just like the last time he got lost.

～ ～

It was late fall and I had just turned twelve. Father had not been home for two days and there was nothing to eat in the house. It was snowing when we caught a ride to town with Mrs. Nelson. Mother charged some groceries and we carried them to our car, which was parked in front of the Cenotaph Hotel. We huddled in the car and ate cold weiners while we waited for the beer parlour to close. By the time it did, the storm raged.

The fight started before we left town. "Why the hell did you bring the kids out on a night like this?" he demanded.

"Because there was nothing to eat, you idiot. If you brought home groceries instead of hangovers, I wouldn't have to beg rides to town."

I put my hands over my ears and stared at the snowflakes hitting the window. I could still hear.

"Are you saying I don't provide for my family, Louisa? Is that what you're saying? And don't call me an idiot." He waved his arms.

The car skidded. Mother grabbed the wheel. They wrestled for it and we left the road. The car stopped in the ditch and settled into the soft snow until it was almost covered. We were near our neighbours' and Father walked to their house. They came with a horse and sleigh and took Mother and the twins for the night. Cattle had to be fed in the morning, so Father and I decided to walk home. We wrapped blankets around ourselves and set off across the field.

I kept my head down and followed his footsteps. The wet snow froze my eyes. I trudged behind and held my hands over them until I could see. When I looked down, his footprints had vanished. I'd veered from his tracks. I looked around and called, but there was only the swirling snow.

I wandered for what felt like hours, chilled by wind and fear. Ice entered my belly and frost built up in my bones. I stumbled, got up, and fell again. It happened over and over — stand, walk, fall down; stand, walk, fall down. Each time it took longer to get up. I wanted to stay below the wind, close my eyes, and drift into sleep.

I was bent over, almost crawling, when I bumped into something. The barn! I went in and thawed myself in the warmth of sleeping cattle. When I could feel, I climbed to the loft and shouted for my father.

❧　❧

They stopped the search after a week. The snow fell all that week and hid him until spring. I looked every day and finally found him in April, but coyotes had uncovered him first. What they hadn't wanted was scattered in the melting snow. I gathered him up and brought him home.

I quit school as soon as I was old enough. The twins left when they were sixteen. I haven't heard from them for years. Mother and I ran the farm until she died.

I'm alone here now and I'm afraid I've let things run down. I never seem to have enough time. There are parts of him I haven't found yet, but I'm still looking.

The CENOTAPH

If you pull back the curtain on the south window in the Cenotaph Hotel Beer Parlour, you'll be looking straight at the cenotaph for which the hotel and the beer parlour are named. A cenotaph is a monument erected to the dead but containing no remains. Hank, the owner of the beer parlour, says that describes his business perfectly, even on a good day.

The cenotaph sits at the end of Main Street, surrounded by a low fence. Folks make U-turns in front of it and the brown granite is coated with road dust. It's flanked on two sides by Vickers machine guns, but nowadays the grass isn't cut, so in summer it grows high enough to hide the guns. Occasionally kids write obscenities on the granite but the act itself doesn't desecrate. Defilement is a slow process and needs hatred. The sanctity of the site is really in people's memories.

Carved on all four sides of the cenotaph, and inscribed on honour rolls in each of the United, Anglican and Lutheran churches, are the names of young men from Tuckahoe who died during wars that flared long enough to kill a generation of mother's sons and then faded when politicians found other diversions. The names on each roll depended on which church laid claim to the soul of the dead hero, or at least claimed the allegiance of his parents. The Singing Evangelist Holy Gospel Church on the edge of town is a newcomer and has yet to have a young member of its congregation blown to bits in some foreign country. But like Reverend Davies, the preacher at Holy Gospel, says: "Given the state of the world, it's probably going to happen sooner than later."

On the cenotaph and in every church, one name is conspicuous: Private Dylan Caldwell. Dylan was the only son of Lydia and Gil Caldwell. Lydia raised him on her own after Gil went through the ice and drowned in Blackjacket Lake one cold December morning. Dylan was three at the time.

꿈   꿈

The Caldwells lived in a two room cabin at the far end of the lake close to what is called Shadow Country, a place unaltered from the way God designed it, a place far enough off the prairie that moss and spruce trees defeated sunlight. The dim quietness ensured that the encumbrances of the past stayed in the past. Here, though they wrestled nature for every meal, Gil and Lydia lived in peace without interruption from the outside world.

They didn't completely cut themselves off. Lydia had been raised to respect God and she insisted Gil take her and Dylan to church on Sundays. Never partisan, she became a member of every congregation in town.

The churches were territorial. Each wanted the Caldwells as members and each resented the idea of sharing. Father Merrill approached Lydia about attending the Anglican Church exclusively. "Don't you find it confusing to worship in those places?" he asked. "We're the only ones that conduct ourselves as God intended."

Lydia shrugged her shoulders. "We all get mixed up in the graveyard," she said. "I don't figure when God gets a new soul from Tuckahoe, it'll be stamped *Made in the Anglican Church*."

Lydia was in her prime when Gil died. She was tall, with long brown hair and eyes that mirrored the shadows she lived in. Men of all makes and persuasions snapped their heads around when she went to town for supplies. There were plenty of suitors. When they came calling she turned them down.

"Since Gil cashed in, I got more use for fresh fish than a man's company. What you got, I don't need, unless you caught it in the lake and scaled it before you brought it over." After a while even the most persistent got the message.

Things were not easy for Lydia. To keep herself and Dylan fed she became the town maid. She scrubbed floors, washed other women's clothes, cleaned chicken coops, weeded gardens, gutted fish and cooked meals for hungry bachelors, many of whom felt dessert should be served in the bedroom. The hours were long and most of the work degrading, filthy and mind-numbing.

While working, she left Dylan with her neighbour, Leona Crable. Mrs. Crable was a thin, dry woman with unfocused eyes. Her own son had died as an infant years before. She hid it well, but the loss had caused her world to wobble and she was unbalanced much of the time. Dylan became the hook on which she hung blame. She alternated between resentment and overwhelming love, swaying between smothering Dylan with attention and smothering him with a pillow. On bad days she locked him in a dark root cellar. Sometimes she forced vile things down his throat. Eventually she went too far. Obsessed with cleanliness, she bathed him in scalding water. From then on, Lydia took her son with her when she worked.

Unfortunately the burns on Dylan's body weren't the only damage. Scar tissue grew around his spirit. He became a sullen, morose child, prone to rage and invective, his face frozen into a sneer. Only near Lydia did his manner lighten and his features relax. Away from her, there were problems.

At Sunday school the complaints were many. He was undisciplined and disrupted class. He didn't respect teachers or church property. He was insolent and answered back. The more tangible of his crimes ranged from biting Father Merrill's thumb to drinking sacramental wine.

Tuckahoe's Sunday school teachers didn't have the patience or temperament for Dylan and his shenanigans. As Nancy Ross put it to her friend Jessica Austin one day after church, "Every time Dylan's in my class, I feel like the Devil's winning."

"Amen," Jessica said. "I keep expecting the kid to grow a tail and sprout horns. Mark my words, that boy will burn one day."

One by one the churches expelled Dylan from their Sunday schools.

He fared no better in public school. In the first hour of Grade One he aimed a slingshot and hit Mrs. Golden on her behind — a painful experience for Mrs. Golden, as her behind was ample and her skirt stretched tight across it. The shot produced a loud thwack. The shooter found this so satisfying that he gave himself up to wild laughter.

Mr. Trimble, the principal, had a fearsome reputation. He was a big man with piercing eyes that looked right through a misbehaving student. Thick black eyebrows stood out from his face. When he scowled, furrows drifted across his forehead like waves on a stormy sea. An African war-club and a replica of a Japanese sword hung on the wall behind his desk.

All the students knew that Mr. Trimble warned you *once*. The next time you got the strap. If the lesson went unlearned, he beat you to death with the war club and then used the sword to cut up your body so it could be removed without being conspicuous. Proof was in one simple fact: there were no students in the school who had ever survived a war-club beating.

Mr. Trimble picked up the leather strap and tapped it on the palm of his hand as he remonstrated with Dylan. "Young man, in this school we respect teachers and we certainly don't shoot them in the backside with slingshots." He scowled until the wrinkles moved on his forehead. Dylan responded by kicking him on the shin.

The principal summoned Lydia. "It's the unanimous opinion of the teaching staff that Dylan isn't ready for school," he said, rubbing his shin and dragging on a cigarette. "It would be better if you kept him out and tried again next year."

Lydia taught him at home and he proved capable. He learned to read, write and do sums. The next year she extracted a promise of good behaviour before bringing Dylan to school. The promise was a temporary success. Dylan lasted a few years before he was sent home for fighting with Dennis Kyle, the school bully — a fight that culminated in Dennis being shoved through the hole in the seat of the school outhouse. Dennis was a slow learner and the act was repeated a number of times, until he grew too large to fit through the hole. The teachers took a dim view of fighting and eventually Dylan was permanently expelled — barred from ever entering the school again. The expulsion was not popular with the smaller students, because Dennis Kyle immediately resumed all the activities that had previously made their school lives a living hell.

Mr. Trimble told Lydia, "It's not that we think Dylan can't learn, but he spends his time fighting and we can't allow that. He shoved the Kyle boy down the toilet at least three times and Dennis Kyle's father is on the school board! Also Dylan's teacher finds it impossible to write on the board and cover her behind at the same time. I can't allow him through the door again. He ignites trouble in every class he's in."

Lydia also taught Dylan what she knew of hunting and fishing. What she couldn't teach, he learned from Indian and Métis trappers. What they couldn't teach, the bush taught on its own. He learned to decoy a duck and hit a grouse on the fly. He taught himself to skin beaver and snare rabbits. He roamed from one end of the back country to the other, ranging over miles of escarpment, eating what he shot and what he caught. The lakes, rivers, and pine trees were better stocked than grocery stores for those who knew how to shop them. Dylan found the bargains: mature hazelnuts, the sweetest blueberries, succulent pickerel and melt-in-your-mouth venison. Occasionally he tramped far onto the prairie, where he became equally at ease with open horizons and miles of waving grass.

Dylan was a teen when Lydia began to suffer periods of illness followed by episodes of extreme weariness. By this time his trap line supported the two of them. He worked long days and built a wall of independence around their lives. It wasn't uncommon, if the moon was bright, to hear the thud of his axe into the early hours as he felled trees for winter fires.

"I swear you'll never have to work for other people again," he told his mother. "The bastards can clean up their own filth." But work was not an option for Lydia. As time passed, her illness became severe and she spent long periods confined to the cabin.

Work provided security and a sense of permanence, while life in the bush and sleeping under the stars embedded in the boy's soul the idea that nothing in this world is permanent, except perhaps the stars themselves. This curious anomaly was natural for those whose backyard contained both the timeless rock of the Canadian Shield and the pale, fleeting beauty of a prairie rose.

The land provided in direct proportion to the effort expended. By his late teens, Dylan was the best trapper and hunter for miles. He never failed to bag what he went after. Men came to hunt with him and learn his secrets. No one went twice. Most found tracking a deer twenty miles, shooting it, butchering it and packing it home an unpleasant way to spend the day. For Dylan Caldwell, it was normal.

One month before his twentieth birthday, the nation went to war. He was now a tall, unsmiling man with black hair and cold eyes. The army drafted him and he left Tuckahoe on an eastbound midnight train, carrying his rifle under his long buckskin coat. He told Lydia he would return to look after her and he did — the next day on the westbound train.

It was the first of many times Dylan would go AWOL. The military police soon learned the way to Lydia's cabin and he was always picked up within days.

Dylan was stubborn but the army proved his equal. After each trip home he spent a longer period behind bars. When he emerged, he marched for a few days and disappeared again. The army gained on him, however. There came a day when he finished basic training. His fellow recruits were ecstatic. They were going overseas to join the war. A party was thrown to celebrate their impending departure. Dylan missed the party. He was hitchhiking home to Tuckahoe. By this time he had been labelled an unrepentant coward by everyone from his C.O. to his fellow soldiers.

The army came for him again. This time he was nowhere to be found. Folks knew he was in the neighbourhood. Though she was sick and frail, Lydia had started selling large numbers of beaver and muskrat pelts.

Some of Tuckahoe's parents received notice of dead sons. Folks started to remember Dylan. In the Cenotaph Hotel Beer Parlour, venom flowed like piss from a race horse. Ancient one-legged Andrew Kyle, whose grandson, Dennis, was in uniform, said, "Dylan Caldwell's as yellow as shit from a sick calf, and he's a disgrace to the country, the army and the town. He dirties up the name of all the boys who are dying over there. They ought to shoot him and put him out of his misery. If I was younger, I'd do it myself."

No one in the beer parlour disagreed. Everyone thought it was just a matter of time. Too many people were willing to put Dylan out of his misery.

Dylan moved farther into the back country and was rarely seen. Occasionally, when Lydia was too sick to make the trip, he slipped into town dressed in his buckskin coat. He traded pelts for staples. As Theo Stone, who sold groceries in front and bought fur in the back, said, "It ain't likely I'm going to tell him to take his business elsewhere when he's toting that rifle of his."

The army's attention was diverted by the war and the matter of Dylan was left in the hands of the local police. They knew how handy he was with a rifle. Consequently, time passed and he was not pursued. The war started to wind down. Things quietened. When Dylan's name was brought up folks still commented on the softness of his spine or the colour of his belly, but no one organised a hunting party.

The end of the war brought new information and more gaps in the town's population. One by one, names were added to the cenotaph and the church honour rolls.

By now Lydia rarely had the strength to venture out of her cabin. When she did, most folks had the manners not to press for Dylan's whereabouts. A few youngsters threw snowballs and yelled obscenities, but she chose not to hear. One morning she failed to wake up. Dylan found her that afternoon. He buried her and burned the cabin to the ground. Gradually the Caldwells faded into the back of the town's memory. Apart from quick, silent visits to Theo Stone's store, Dylan might not have existed.

Principal Trimble neared the end of his career. He now needed a mid-afternoon nap to get through the school day. If it was a hectic day he sometimes needed two naps. At noon, it was his habit to close his office door, eat the Spam sandwich Mrs. Trimble packed for him, lean back in his large principal's chair, light a cigarette and digest his impending retirement along with the Spam. He then closed his eyes for his daily snooze.

One day he dozed off early. A burning cigarette rolled from his ashtray and came to rest beside a stack of newly prepared report cards. It smouldered there, gradually answering the prayers of all but the best students. It spread to loose papers, licked its way across the desk and shot up the curtain. Mr. Trimble snored as his office became an inferno. By the time smoke entered his nostrils and overwhelmed the lingering taste of Spam, the door was blocked by flames. He grabbed the war club, smashed a window and jumped to safety. Then he raced around the building shouting an alarm. Teachers and students left their classrooms and exited through the back door.

A crowd gathered. Mr. Trimble took a head count. Mrs. Golden and her Grade One class were missing! They were trapped. Mrs. Golden had been overcome by smoke. By now the building looked like the inside of hell itself. The crowd was helpless. Volunteers sprayed small, futile streams of water.

Children's screams were heard from inside and echoed by frantic parents outside. The heat was intense. No one could get close, let alone enter the burning building. It looked ready to collapse.

Suddenly a figure dashed across the street from Theo Stone's store, went through the open door of the school and disappeared into the flames. A few seconds later, a chair was thrown through a side window, followed by a screaming child.

That child was followed by another. One by one the children were dragged to safety. A large woman, wrapped in a buckskin coat, was propelled through the front door at the same moment the building fell on itself. The winter afternoon gave way to evening with sparks still soaring into the darkening sky. It continued until there was little left for flames to feed on.

All thirteen of Mrs. Golden's Grade One students survived, as did Mrs. Golden, thanks to the buckskin protecting her from the flames. Only one body was recovered from the building: Dylan Caldwell's, dressed in what was left of his army uniform.

Private Caldwell's name was added to all the honour rolls in town without telling the army or the government. To this day, few Tuckahoe citizens can look out the south window of the Cenotaph Hotel Beer Parlour without remembering the shadowy figure who threw so many through a school window and into their future.

One More Damn Mistake

It was a bright Sunday afternoon on a dried-out prairie baseball diamond when Pen Peters walked away. Although hundreds saw it, few knew why he did it. Somewhere in shallow left, or maybe just behind second, Pen decided to step away from this town forever.

🙠 🙢

Dust explodes from the wheels of my car, rises high into the blue sky, then settles on the droning prairie like a gritty brown shroud. In the town, fake second floors threaten to fall across Main Street. Twenty years is a long time, but Tuckahoe stays the same — ageless as the land it sits on and stubborn as the folks who live here. The town has no promise. Summer heat and winter ice wear away ambition the way heels give out on old cowboy boots. The dust obscures everything, but sometimes a devil breeze sweeps it away to show the underlying landscape, just as circumstance occasionally shifts a lie to reveal truth.

I was back for the reunion. The town hadn't changed, but Pen had. We ran into each other the first night and were sitting in the Cenotaph Hotel Beer Parlour, drinking and catching up.

"There's lots of water flowed under my bridge, Andy," he said. "Time rolls past when you stand still. Things ain't like they used to be." His voice was a mixture of nicotine, whiskey and self-pity. His hand shook when he lifted his glass.

"Geez Pen, what happened? You don't look so good, if you don't mind me saying."

I was being kind. He looked like hell. He'd always lived hard and it had caught up with him. A biography of booze and late nights was written on his unshaven face. His stomach hid his belt. Youth had fled along with his blond curly hair. There were no souvenirs. Once, he owned everything between second and third, and held a mortgage on shallow left. All he had left was his nickname.

His real name was Lonnie, but he'd been called Pen since Little League. It was short for Penguin. With a glove on, he floated over ground like balloons at the fair. He could read a ball's mind and was always there waiting when it got where it was going. On the base path he was fast, but he wasn't pretty. His toes pointed out. He never failed to end up where he was headed, but folks said he ran like a penguin. The name stuck.

"Things ain't worked the way I hoped, Andy." He stared at the floor and mumbled into the top of his shirt. "You know me and Joanne got married after you split."

"I know. What happened? I heard there were problems. You didn't have any kids, did you, Lonnie?" It didn't seem right to call him Pen when he was down.

"You're right about problems. No, she didn't stick around long enough for kids. She left before the season was over. Guess she didn't like me away all the time. I wasn't good at getting home, even when I could have. Just one more damn mistake. My life's full of them."

I looked at him close. This wasn't the Pen I remembered. Everything about him shouted *loser*. Andy and Pen, we'd been a team — a winning team. We'd known each other from the beginning: grown up together, got our first ball gloves at the same time and played the six-four combo through school, on into that glorious summer when we hooked up with a bigger town's hired team and actually got paid to do what we loved.

I'd been a fair second baseman and Pen was a superb shortstop. He patrolled the line like a bloodhound and could dig out anything low and heading to left. We turned some of the prettiest double plays you ever saw. Unlike me, he was an all-round player. He could bunt, hit where he wanted, and he ran bases smarter than anybody. Once he was on, catchers gave him second, even with his funny run.

No matter how hard I worked, I didn't have what came to him naturally. I finally quit and went off to college. After a few false starts I ended up in my present job, chief accountant for a down-east utility. I hadn't stepped on to a diamond once in twenty years.

Pen said he'd done it different. He bummed around, playing anywhere someone would give him work so he could help a local team. Now he did odd jobs, earning only enough for food, booze and the price of admission to a ball park.

"She went to live with that son of a bitch, Slip Frame," Pen said. "He was a bastard then and I hear he ain't changed." He took a drink and made a face. It was probably the memory that tasted bad. The beer seemed okay.

Pen was right. Slip was a bastard. His family owned Frame Brothers' Seed Plant and most of the other businesses in town. Slip always got what he wanted. He was big and a bully when we were kids. No one beat him at anything. Ever since I could remember, he was jealous of Pen's ball playing and he chased Joanne, Pen's girlfriend, all through high school. She and Pen had been so much in love; I was surprised they broke up. I was more surprised about her and Slip. They didn't fit together; it was like mixing scotch and root beer.

Joanne was the prettiest girl in high school. The three of us were inseparable. She didn't just taste life, she ate it up. She had it all — looks, personality, and she was smart. She laughed a lot and folks just naturally felt good when she was around. When she had an idea her blonde pony tail bounced with excitement, and we held our breath when she explained her plans.

"Let's swim in Mr. James's dugout." And we'd play hooky and splash the afternoon away.

"Let's get crabapples." And we'd creep into Mr. Cleary's yard and strip his tree.

"Let's go fishing." And we'd pedal the dusty road all the way to Blackjacket Lake.

We lazed away entire summer afternoons swimming, riding horses and talking baseball. At night we watched falling stars and stole from gardens. Pen worshipped her. He would have joined a church if she asked. Together they were a team. When they were apart, he fell apart. She kept him running smooth like a spark plug keeps an engine from sputtering.

While I adored her, I wasn't jealous. I never imagined any other combination except her and Pen. They were as natural as a double play from Tinker to Evers to Chance.

"Yeah, I had to leave town permanent," Pen said. "I gambled back then and I was always broke. I ended up owing Slip and his uncle tons of money. They owned me — wanted me to work off my debts in their goddam plant. I had to leave. I couldn't face working for the prick. Not after he got Joanne, anyway. I ain't been back since. I still owe the money. Difference is, now I don't care. The only reason I'm here is to see how Joanne is."

"I think you're going to get your chance," I said.

A bunch of people had entered the bar. It wasn't hard to spot Slip and Joanne. He was tall with slick, black, shiny hair. I had to admit he looked good. But if he looked good, then Joanne looked terrific. She hadn't changed a bit. She was tall, blonde, slim and still had curves a pitcher would die for.

She was laughing and joking as they came through the door. When she saw Pen, it was like she got shot. She stopped dead and her mouth fell open. Slip looked over. I could tell he recognized us. His face twisted and he jerked Joanne's arm. She stumbled and followed him to the other side of the bar, her hand covering her mouth.

Lonnie had spilled his beer. I thought I better change the subject. "You seen any of the other guys?" I asked. "How about Gabby Cleary? Remember the time he pitched drunk? And with no sleep, too."

We replayed the story. Somebody had spotted Gabby parked with his girlfriend behind the dance hall at seven AM. We poured coffee in him, slapped him around, dressed him in his uniform and had him on the mound for the first pitch of a tournament at nine. After he walked the first three batters he settled down, or sobered up, or both, and allowed only one other player to reach first for the rest of the game. We won, four – zip.

Pen straightened up when we started talking about the old days, although he kept looking across the room. Some of our old teammates came in. Soon there were seven of us sitting around telling lies. We rehashed it all, from Little League through our crackerjack high school team. We talked about the time I was spiked at second and still turned the double play that ended a ninth inning rally, the first of three regional championships. And about the time we recruited Pen's visiting cousin, who had played Triple A. He threw every game of a tournament. One was a no-hitter. His status as the best ringer ever was uncontested.

It had been the golden age of prairie baseball. The bigger towns hired players to supplement local boys who were long on desire and short on talent. Most hired players were outcasts from the Negro Leagues, but sometimes a town would field shiny-faced college kids from California. Occasionally a Cuban or Mexican would show up, shivering in somebody's outfield.

Barnstorming teams with colourful names like the Florida Eagles or Texas Steers worked their way from tournament to tournament, trying to earn enough to eat. We talked about watching Satchel Paige, and the time Pen was picked to play against the touring Kansas City Monarchs, and the time he homered against a bearded House of David pitcher.

He quit mumbling in his shirt. The present disappeared. We remembered and he responded. He wasn't a loser. He was his best performances. He laughed. He joked. He picked his gaze off the floor and looked us in the eye. We forgot jobs and mortgages and travelled back. It was exhilarating . . . until the bubble shattered.

As the evening wore on, we'd got louder. Some local lads sensed sport and moved in. "Just a bunch of old drunk has-beens," a pimply-faced farm boy ventured, loud enough for us to hear.

"Go to hell," Pen answered, feisty as he'd been at twenty.

"Look at him," Pimples said in a stage whisper. "Not only is he drunk and fat and bald, he's got a big mouth. Probably figures he can still play ball."

"Button it up kid," Caver Speight spoke quietly, "or I'll kick your ass so hard you'll need to take off your shirt to have a shit." Caver got his name by caving in skulls at Saturday night dances, but that was twenty years ago. Now he had arthritis and a beer gut. None of the kids looked threatened.

"Another has-been," jeered Pimples. "All mouth and nothing behind it. I bet none of you old jerks can catch a ball anymore . . . if you ever could."

Pen bristled. "Listen, you rotten little piece of afterbirth. Me and the guys got twice what it takes to kick the crap out of any fuzzy-cheeked pukes you can put together. Put up or shut up, shit-for-brains."

A blond, good-looking kid stood up. "Put a cork in it, Pops," he said. "You got no right to talk to my friends like that. You're nothing, a big zero, a top to bottom phoney. If you got the guts, bring your has-been friends and show up Sunday. We'll cream you on the field. Maybe I'll do it right here, too." He waved his fist under Pen's nose.

I expected Pen to come up swinging, but he just looked at the floor. "Maybe kid," he said. "Just maybe."

They started to leave, laughing and looking back. Most were just having fun, but the blond kid oozed hostility as he stared at Pen. "Just wait 'til Sunday, you old bastard," he said. "We'll murder you."

He tramped over and sat with Slip and Joanne. Pen didn't say anything, just stayed slumped in his chair.

Caver whispered in my ear. "That's Slip and Joanne's kid, Michael. He knows Pen was married to his mom. Since day one, Slip's poisoned him against Pen."

We were quiet after they left. The mood was gone. Nobody said anything. Slip got up from his table and came across the room. "Looks like you're going to play my team," he said. "I'm the boys' coach. Michael told me all about it. I've decided to stick it to you jokers. It's time the lies stopped. Me and the kids are going to show the town just what bull crap we been hearing for years. You especially, Penguin. By the time we're finished with you, there'll only be a little smear for dogs to lick."

⚐ ⚑

We were short two players. We got a pitcher from one of the nearby towns, a nephew of Doug, our balding first baseman. The other volunteer was Roy, a local who was older than any of us, but looked in better shape. We put him in the outfield.

We went three up, three down to start. I was nervous when we took the field, but Doug's nephew had good speed, which kept the kids off the scoreboard and us in the game. We had no better luck against their pitcher, but a walk and a couple of errors got us to the bottom of the ninth, up 1-0.

It was like old times. Twice, balls were hammered to me on the path. I fished them out and backhanded to Pen. He wheeled, brushed second, jumped the spikes and dealt to first. Perfect! We were back. The double plays and our one run gave us confidence. Suddenly we knew we could win. Trepidation became jubilation. The dugout was a time machine, and the ride back was glorious.

Slip, on the other side of the field, looked glummer as the game moved along. He swore a lot, but saved his best venom for Pen. "Hey Penguin, you fat loser," he yelled. "Back up from the plate. Your gut's filling the strike zone."

Pen gritted his teeth and stared at the pitcher, but his eye wasn't working. He couldn't get wood on the ball. That was a surprise, but one thing hadn't changed. Even though Slip had it all, he was still jealous of Pen.

I looked behind the dugout where Joanne was sitting. She was pert and pretty in a yellow summer dress. Her chin rested in her hand. She was staring at Pen, lost in a daydream. *Damn,* I thought. *She still loves him. Even though she sleeps in Slip's bed, it's still Pen. That's what all this is about.*

We took the field. Things started okay. Doug's nephew struck out the first batter. Then he walked Pimples. Michael came to the plate. He fouled off a couple and then hit a sharp roller to right. I scooted left, plucked it out of the dirt, and flipped it to Pen at second. The ball crossed the bag, drifted down, and rolled to a stop on the outfield grass. Pen wasn't at second! He was twenty feet away! He hadn't moved! He was watching Michael as he turned at first.

Everyone started yelling. Roy came huffing in, aiming at the ball, sitting white as a lie, in short centre. Pimples crossed the plate. I watched Michael round third, carrying home the winning run. He was moving fast. With his toes pointed out he looked just like a penguin.

Pen dropped his glove, turned, and walked across second. He passed me without looking, eyes empty as an August slough. "Just one more damn mistake," I heard him mutter. He went past the dugout, by the line of parked cars, and onto the road out of town. No one ever saw him again.

The DAY HELL FROZE OVER

Hell froze over on the same hot, stifling Sunday in August that Scowling Judd Pikebender married Lorena Clammerhorn in the Singing Evangelist Holy Gospel Church of the Infinite Redeemer in the town of Tuckahoe, Saskatchewan. The two events were not unconnected. The story was related to me by Jeremy Pikebender, the only child of Judd and Lorena. I record it for you exactly as Jeremy told it to me. Any deviation from what actually occurred is probably due to the way the tale was edited when it was passed on to him by his parents. Whether you see the story as uplifting, depressing or even spiritual depends entirely on what you're drinking when you read it.

Tuckahoe is a town that has evolved in its own special way because almost the entire population of the rest of the world is unaware of its existence. This allows the inhabitants to go about their business without worrying what others think of them, except of course, for the citizens who have relatives in far away places like Moose Jaw or Medicine Hat. As a consequence, people in Tuckahoe have developed the habit of doing exactly what they want, when they want and how they want.

The highway into town is the highway out of town, which causes folks in neighbouring communities to say that Tuckahoe is the end of the road. This is unkind because the town has *attributes*: a stockyard; five grain elevators; a hotel with a beer parlour; two cafés (one of which is patronized); a school which contains twelve grades, some with pupils; a couple of general stores; four churches.

Holy Gospel, the newest church, was founded by the late Robert B. Hermanutz who used to harangue folks on the street in front of Louie's Café every Saturday night after he got a snoot full. Eventually he quit drinking, turned the harangues into sermons and put up a tent at the end of Main Street. When his congregation outgrew the tent, they moved to a building on the edge of town that once housed a Cockshutt Machinery dealership. Beneath the original sign, which depicted a tractor pulling a cultivator, Robert painted the slogan, *"Ploughing in the Fields of the Lord"*. The current preacher is Robert's nephew, the Reverend Jason Davies. Before Robert died, he declared himself a Pastor, thus creating a position for his nephew to inherit. The position caused Jason to alter his career path. In order to assume his ecclesiastical duties, he gave up selling tobacco products in the schoolyard. But I'm getting ahead of myself. Pastor Hermanutz was very much alive when the events I'm about to relate took place.

The Pikebenders and Clammerhorns are two of the oldest families in the district, and both belong to Holy Gospel. At the time of our story, Mr. and Mrs. Pikebender had gone the way of all flesh, leaving behind four sons, each of whom sported clear blue eyes, brown wavy hair and a square jaw. The responsibility for running the family farm had migrated to the shoulders of the two oldest, Judd and Jack.

There were five Clammerhorn girls. All had been raised by old B.P. Clammerhorn after his wife died of heat prostration while taking part in a wild-cow-milking contest at the summer fair. After her mother's death, the oldest daughter, Lorena, took charge of the household.

The two families generally ignored each other. One exception was the occasion when the Clammerhorn's scrub bull marched through a fence and became carnally involved with a number of Pikebender dairy cows. The offspring from the liaison refused to put on weight and produced no milk. They did produce bad blood, however, and were a constant burr under the Pikebender saddle. Notwithstanding this, Judd Pikebender and Lorena Clammerhorn were able to develop a relationship, not unlike the one that had precipitated the bad blood in the first place.

The story of how Judd and Lorena came to be man and wife started on a July afternoon in front of Louie's Café. The usual crowd was holding up Louie's walls and keeping the sidewalk flat. A few lazy flies buzzed under the awning, and a lone dragonfly idled in the sun. Judd's brother, Smiling Jack Pikebender, entertained the crowd by making rude noises utilizing his left hand and his right armpit. He was intent on his performance and failed to notice that one member of his audience wasn't laughing. Old B.P. Clammerhorn had a look of serious purpose when he stepped in front of Jack. He glared until Jack took his hand from his armpit and glared back. Minutes passed. The dragonfly got bored and flew away.

Mr. Clammerhorn towered over Jack. He never told anybody what B.P. stood for, but behind his back, most folks referred to him as Big Prick. He broke the silence. "My daughter's pregnant," he said. "When is your brother planning to do the honourable thing and marry my little girl?"

Jack allowed a grin to creep over his perpetual smile as he spoke to all present. "My brother would sooner hang his balls in boiling oil than marry a Clammerhorn," he said. "From what I hear, getting Lorena pregnant was a lot like running the railroad. It wasn't a one man job."

B.P. took a moment to digest this heresy and then decided that boiling oil was too good for Jack or his brother. So he shot Jack. Fortunately, B.P.'s eyesight wasn't what it used to be and the bullet lodged in the south portion of his left buttock. Also fortunate was the fact that B.P. had been potting gophers and so was carrying only a single shot rabbit gun with a .22 calibre short in it. Another reason Jack was fortunate was that he decided to run as soon as he realized B.P. was about to shoot, which was why the .22 short landed in the fattest part of his rear machinery. Even with all these fortunates, it was a number of weeks before he was able to sit at a table in the beer parlour, or walk without limping to the piss shack behind the Cenotaph Hotel.

Scowling Judd Pikebender was a hothead. The shooting of his brother increased the temperature in his braincase to the level of cerebral inferno — a level that left no alternative but to douse it with a bucket of revenge.

He didn't have long to wait. B.P. spent much of his time in the beer parlour, anaesthetizing the sympathy pains he felt for his pregnant, unmarried daughter. One day Judd followed him when he went to the piss shack. While B.P. was in deep concentration at the trough, Judd hit him with a bottle.

B.P.'s head was solid. The bottle broke, causing an ugly wound. Though momentarily staggered, his hard head protected him from a concussion. He blinked his eyes, grabbed Judd's throat, and squeezed until Judd was in danger of leaving this world with a purple hue on his scowl. He then positioned Judd's head in the trough and held it while he pulled the chain on the flushing mechanism. The water cooled Judd's brain and diluted the purplish hue.

"The little snot tried to brain me," B.P. told Lorena as she washed dried blood from his craggy features. "I don't care if you are knocked up; you can't marry the son-of-a-bitch now."

"Yes, Papa," Lorena said, pushing a needle and harness thread through the gash on the old man's head.

Judd retired to the farm to lick his wounds. After they had been licked, he made a trip to Tuckahoe, where he marched up and down Main Street and publicly swore to make B.P. the next member of the mouldering fraternity in the graveyard. The fact that he did it while sober showed he meant it. Jack limped behind and proclaimed his willingness to assist his brother.

B.P. adopted a more conciliatory tone. "I shouldn't have taken exception to Smiling Jack's statement," he told the crowd in front of Louie's. "There's never been a Pikebender with any balls to boil in oil."

At this point, Pastor Hermanutz began to worry. The competition between the churches was fierce. There were barely enough parishioners to go around and some of his own were threatening to do each other in. Besides, how did it look — Lorena getting bigger each week and coming to church with no husband? He decided to ask God's advice. "Lord," he said, "I don't have to tell You this town is small. You can hardly say it has a population, and only a few of them come to my church. It ain't good to have Holy Gospel folks killing each other, especially when the cause is two of my parishioners putting the cart before the horse . . . if You know what I mean. Level with me Lord, and excuse the expression, but how do I keep them from blowing each other to hell?"

The Lord thought long and hard and came up with a plan. He told Pastor Hermanutz to talk sense to both sides. The Pastor thought the Lord might be onto something and started with Smiling Jack. "It was God that made B.P.'s bullet hit your ass instead of a more sensitive part of your anatomy," he said. "And God wants you to quit all this nonsense about getting even."

"But . . . " Jack said, "if we don't stop B.P., he's just going to shoot again, the next time somebody knocks up one of his daughters. I'm sure nobody, including you and the Lord, wants that. Do you, sir?"

Next he talked to B.P. "You're old," he said. "It won't be long until you meet God face to face. If you don't want Him to call off the meeting, you better not shoot any more Pikebenders. Instead, you should help me get those kids married."

B.P. shook his head. "I been speaking to God myself, Reverend. He told me He don't want no more Pikebenders waving their peckers around my girls, so unless hell freezes over, there ain't going to be no wedding."

Pastor Hermanutz revisited the Lord. "I don't know what else to do," he said. "I've tried but I'm not getting through. It's like the devil's putting excuses in their mouths. Unless You're about to drop the temperature 'til Satan wears long johns, I don't see any way. I need more help."

But the Lord was silent and Pastor Hermanutz began to think he'd been abandoned. A sliver of doubt took root in him. Maybe God was on the other side. Maybe He was a Lutheran, or an Anglican, or, horror-of-horrors, a Catholic. He shivered. It wasn't possible . . . but still . . .

Pastor Hermanutz became depressed, but he needn't have worried. The Lord was just taking His time while He figured out in what mysterious way He was going to move in order to perform a wonder. In the meantime, Lorena's indiscretion became more visible every day.

But depression wasn't the Pastor's forte. Preaching was. With a Herculean effort, he pulled himself together. If he couldn't get Judd and Lorena married, at least he could put on a show no other church could match. Maybe a good show would bring folks together. He spread the word that big things were going to happen.

On Sunday, there was standing room only. Lutherans and Anglicans were scattered among the regulars. Even a few Catholics sidled through the door and clung warily to the back wall. The Pikebenders and Clammerhorns sat on opposite sides of the church. Lorena, well into her eighth month, took a front row seat. The other Clammerhorn girls stuck out their tongues at the Pikebenders and the Pikebenders glowered and swore under their breath.

You could say many things about the Pastor's sermons, but you couldn't call them dull. He'd assembled the best musical talent in Tuckahoe. Peter Paulsen played the accordion and Jenny Dunkle strummed the banjo. Pastor Hermanutz shook a tambourine as he preached, and his wife Cecilia took her usual spot at the piano.

As he got into his sermon his voice took on a commanding, hypnotic tone. He marched back and forth across the front of the church, shook the tambourine, praised God, threatened the devil and cajoled the congregation. The music increased in tempo and volume.

"How many of you listen to the radio?" he shouted. " . . . to the hockey game . . . to baseball . . . to Lux Radio Theater?"

One by one hands rose in the congregation.

"Yes, you listen to the hockey game . . . to Amos and Andy. Then you turn the knob and switch off the radio. Well, Jesus is not your radio. You can't tune to Him for an hour on Sunday, and then shut Him off for the rest of the week."

"Amen, Reverend," a voice shouted from the back.

Pastor Hermanutz was warming up. "No, you can't shut Jesus off. He broadcasts on every frequency. His program is never over. Mathew . . . didn't turn Jesus off. Mark . . . didn't turn Jesus off. Luke . . . didn't turn Jesus off . . . and you shouldn't turn Jesus off either. He's waiting to talk to you."

"Tell it, Reverend," someone yelled. "Say it loud!"

The pastor hit his stride. "Friends, you can't tune out the Lord when it suits you — when you hear something you don't like. A Dodgers' fan doesn't turn off the series when Yogi hits a homer. No, he listens. He knows they'll be back."

Shouting and waving his tambourine, Pastor Hermanutz reached the climax of his sermon. "Brothers and Sisters, tune into God! Dial Jesus and crank up the volume! Praise the Lord and pray with me now!"

"Hallelujah!" the congregation bellowed.

"Glory to God!" Pastor Hermanutz replied.

The hallelujahs and praises rang to the rafters and reverberated back to the floor of the old Cockshutt building. Folks swayed in their seats, then stood and clapped. Cecilia sang and pounded the piano. Pastor Hermanutz jumped on a chair and threw off his jacket. Little Henry Donkers shouted, "I'm tunin' in. I hear Him comin'!" and started dancing. Others joined. Fat Janet Petherwick cried, "Yes, yes, Lord Almighty," and fell to the floor, sweating and shaking. Diddly Tompkins leapt about the room, sobbing and shouting, "I'm a sinner. Speak to me, Jesus!"

In the din of the clapping, the singing, the music, and the shouting, Pastor Hermanutz fixed his eyes on each member of his flock. "Open your heart and be saved," he commanded.

Lorena Clammerhorn screamed and slipped to the floor crying. "She's accepted Jesus," the Pastor shouted. "Thank you, Lord."

It was then that Lorena's water broke, and just like that she was giving birth. The Pastor saw. In a flash of insight so brilliant he later decided the finger of God had pointed straight at him, he knew what he had to do. He instructed the musicians to keep playing and told Cecilia to attend to Lorena. Singing and clapping, he made his way to where Judd Pikebender was standing.

"God's talking to you, boy. You understand?" he shouted into Judd's ear. "The Lord has chosen to show you the birth of your child. In a minute, he's going to come into this world a bastard. Only you can prevent that. I can marry you now."

Judd was confused and unsure. His square jaw hung slack, his blue eyes were vacant and his brown hair dishevelled. Pastor Hermanutz took his hand and led him across the floor. Working quickly, he went through the *Do you's* and the *I do's*. He got to the pronouncement part just as Jeremy Pikebender, howling bloody murder, slid into the world and onto the floor of the Singing Evangelist Holy Gospel Church of the Infinite Redeemer in Tuckahoe, Saskatchewan.

Judd stared at Lorena. Lorena, eyes filled with love, stared at her new baby. The baby wailed. In hell, Satan hugged himself to keep warm.

B.P. looked at his new grandson. He felt the hand of the Lord propel him forward. He slapped Judd on the back. "Welcome to the family, son," he said.

STUDSY *and the* INFERNO

This is the story of how my wife, the mother of my children, and I, the father of my children, decided to rekindle our relationship, which was becoming cold and stagnant as a result of my working long hours in Mr. Hackenbrook's egg candling factory, long hours that were necessary because my wife insisted that we move to a new house because the one we were living in was too small and unfit for habitation. When the mother of my children deems something unfit, there is no alternative but to work hard to correct the situation.

The new house was first suggested by the mother of my wife who is the grandmother of my children, and who has made other suggestions concerning both the way we live and the inadequacy of myself as a provider for my children, for the mother of my children and for the grandmother of my children, for of course, she lives with us, which is one of the reasons the house has become too small and unfit for habitation. Her suggestions focus on my inability to supply her with adequate funds to cover her frequent cribbage losses and subsequent shopping excursions, which she takes to forget the humiliation of losing to her friends at a game in which she claims proficiency.

The father of my wife, who is the grandfather of my children, also lives with us, but he limits his activities to trips between the kitchen table and my easy chair, where he reads the same newspaper many times, rolls his eyes toward heaven and takes deep breaths. He never talks to me, but will occasionally grunt when he wants something. The grandmother of my children also does not speak to me, preferring to relay tidings concerning my stupidity through my wife, who is content to be a transmitter of messages. Occasionally she will add an idea of her own, but generally her thoughts vary little from those of her mother.

My wife's parents moved to Tuckahoe and became our permanent house guests two years ago, shortly after the grandfather of my children invested all his money in a scheme to crossbreed a mink and a kangaroo so as to produce a fur coat with pockets.

The sister of my wife, who is my children's aunt, also stays in our house. Her marriage failed because her husband ran away after it was discovered he had a sexual relationship with the young man in Stoneboat Creek who was his wife's hairdresser. Unlike her parents, she does not hesitate to converse with me, sometimes spending hours discoursing on the perfidiousness of men. She has forgiven her hairdresser because, as she says, "One can always find a husband, but when it comes to a good hairdresser, sometimes you just have to suck it up." She has four children, which means her husband wasn't always attracted to young men. It also means that our house is so crowded I must sleep on the veranda, which was fine in the summer but is uncomfortable in cold weather.

I told my wife I liked sleeping with her and missed our activities in the bedroom. She said I shouldn't complain — if I wasn't such a simpleton, we would be in a bigger house and I wouldn't have to sleep on the veranda. Moreover, if her family heard me complain, they might feel bad. When I said that I wouldn't worry if her family felt bad, she explained that it was more fun to sleep with a hot water bottle than with me because a hot water bottle is silent and doesn't have hands.

We were not always like this. Our relationship was like a curtain in an open window. It would blow into many different shapes, but when the breeze stopped it always fell back to what it was — and at one time, it was warm and beautiful. In those days, the mother of my children called me Studsy. But I don't think of that as completely gone. Late at night, on the veranda, when I am missing the comfort of my bed, I think of it as a campfire that has fizzled, leaving the ashes cold. Even though she no longer calls me Studsy, I'm sure if we sifted the ashes we could find a spark. I imagine what it would be like to fan the spark . . . not into an inferno — the days of infernos are gone for us. Just a small flame would be nice.

So when Mr Hackenbrook asked me to represent the company at the annual convention of the International Association of Egg Candlers in a city almost two hundred miles away, I saw an opportunity to be alone with the mother of my children, to look for the spark, and to sleep in a warm place for a change.

The convention had promise. It was in a first-class hotel. There was a welcoming cocktail party and a banquet with entertainment. My expense allowance was generous, my time commitment was not great and the city had many attractions.

At first my wife declined to go because she did not want to leave her mother. I didn't understand this, because her mother is as healthy as two horses. But she was worried her sister might use the opportunity to make sure that my wife was left out in the cold when the mother made a will. I pointed out two things. First, her mother didn't have anything to put in a will, and second, *I* was the only one out in the cold.

Finally she decided to accompany me. Her decision was only a formality; the issue had already been decided by her mother, who wanted me away when she hosted a meeting of her Saturday night cribbage gang. She said the only thing better than two hundred miles between us would be for me to contract a fatal disease.

The mother of my wife also suggested we go by train. She said the trip was only four hours long and it would be healing for my obnoxious personality. I did not disagree. Relaxing in the club car, watching the scenery, toasting each other with fancy drinks and feasting in elegance in the dining car would be important first steps toward locating the missing spark. I told Mr. Hackenbrook I would go, bought rail tickets and in a flash of romantic inspiration booked the Aloha Suite, which, according to the hotel brochure, was sure to kindle notions of love and inspire hours of exotic pleasure.

As we left the house, my mother-in-law was singing to herself — something I hadn't heard since last winter when I fell and broke my leg. We arrived at the station and found our train was late. My wife's shoulders became stiff and she studied a movie magazine for the next two hours. When the train arrived, we boarded the passenger car and found we were the only travellers. I stowed my suitcase on the luggage rack but left my wife's at the end of the car, because it was too large to lift. The mother of my children is a good planner and thinks of every contingency. She'd even packed a black dress in case someone should die and we needed to attend a funeral.

When we sat down, clouds of dust sprang up from the seats and floated the length of the car, each speck visible in the afternoon sun shining through the dirty windows. My wife held a handkerchief to her face but it didn't prevent a fit of choking. She was still coughing when a man in oily coveralls walked through the car. "Where can we get a drink and where's the dining car?" I asked.

He looked at me in the manner of my wife's mother — as though I were unable to go to the bathroom by myself. Then he laughed. "This is a freight train," he said. "We added this car because you bought tickets. You're the first passengers in months. Nobody rides this line anymore. There is no dining car, no drinks, and no food." He walked away chuckling.

My wife's shoulders stiffened again and she held her mouth in a straight line. Staring at me, she used her hat pin to poke holes through a man's picture on the cover of the movie magazine.

In this fashion we passed the time of the trip, which was longer than four hours because we stopped at various locations while the train added and subtracted cars. I rubbed a small hole in the dirt on the window to watch the passing scenery. It took my mind off the hat pin. When the sun went down I saw the city lights. We came to a stop and the man in oily coveralls reappeared. "End of the line folks. You get off here," he said.

"But we're not downtown," I answered.

"This is a freight. We don't go downtown. We're in the rail yard at the edge of the city," he explained.

I carried the bags. Everything was locked and dark. We trudged along a dirt road while my wife spoke encouragement by spelling out my fate should I damage her suitcase. I looked in vain for a taxi. When we came to a residential neighbourhood, I knocked at a house and asked to use the phone, but the lady slammed the door in my face.

After an hour we found a corner store and called a cab, which worked its way through traffic and deposited us at the hotel. I dragged the suitcases to the front desk. The clerk smirked at me. "You're hours late," he said. "Your room wasn't confirmed. We gave it away a long time ago."

"Then give me another room," I said.

"We're filled with egg candlers. I'm sorry, but there's nothing available." He did not appear sorry.

My wife's heels clicked as she marched back and forth in the centre of the lobby. I handed the clerk a twenty. "You have to find a room," I said. "It's worth my life."

He pocketed the twenty. "There is a conference room," he said. "We can roll cots in. It has a basin and toilet but no bath. You'll have to be out before eight. There's a meeting in the morning."

I glanced at the mother of my children pacing like a bear in a cage. It was probably the light, but it looked like steam was rising from the back of her neck. "We'll take it," I said.

We rode the elevator. The bellhop opened the door, dropped our suitcases and held out his hand.

"What the . . . ," my wife exploded. The mother of my children doesn't use foul language but she was close. The bell hop looked at her face and ran.

"They gave away our room," I explained. "This is all that's left."

"The cold weather has frozen your brain. I'm not sleeping here." She marched into the toilet.

There was a phone on a table in the corner. On my sixth call I was successful — a Holiday Inn on the other side of town.

I knocked and told my wife. After a wait, during which I heard glass breaking, she emerged and paraded out the door. I grabbed the suitcases and followed. We hailed a cab, and an hour later we were in our new room. The temperature of my wife's personality rose a few degrees. I relaxed. The cocktail party beckoned. Drinks and snacks were exactly what we needed before a late romantic dinner. We returned to our original hotel.

The ballroom was quiet. A man swept the floor. Two ladies gathered glasses and stacked chairs.

"Excuse me. Isn't this where the egg candler's party is supposed to be?" I asked.

"Yes," the man answered. "But it's over. Everyone's gone."

There was nothing for it but to return to the Holiday Inn, where the mother of my children again went into the bathroom. It crossed my mind that we could save money if we rented only bathrooms. I called room service and ordered a bottle of champagne and a late dinner. When my wife came out, I went in to wash. When I returned, she was in bed with her back to me.

I started to take off my clothes. I had no idea it would be this easy to recover the spark. "Dinner is on its way," I said. "Let's share an appetiser before it gets here."

She didn't answer.

"They're bringing champagne." I lifted the blanket and prepared to slide into bed.

She spoke to the wall. "Take your champagne and sleep in the bathtub."

There was a knock on the door. I kept the champagne and sent the dinners back. Then I found a blanket and tried to get comfortable in the tub. I sipped the bubbly liquor and shifted from one side to the other. The tub made my back and neck sore. Sleep was impossible. I started to feel that perhaps, for us, the spark was dead. The more champagne I drank, the deader it became. Finally, close to despair and with my back so sore I could hardly get out of the tub, I decided to go for a walk.

The bar beside the lobby was open. Why not? If I could dull the pain, I might be able to sleep. I went in and ordered a double whiskey.

The drink burned all the way down. I ordered another and looked around. There were two men at the bar. One was tall with a black moustache. "Drowning your sorrows, Mac?" he asked.

"Yes I am," I replied. "The mother of my children told me I had to sleep in a bathtub."

The man laughed. "Sounds serious," he said. "My wife hasn't slept with me for five years. I understand how you feel. Let me buy you a drink."

"Me too," his friend said. "My wife doesn't talk to me."

Two more doubles arrived. They tasted wonderful. Everything was wonderful and the world was marvellous. I forgot about the bathtub and the mother of my children. I bought more whiskey and a round of vodka to return the men's generosity. Then we drank tequila and smoked cigars. Later, we had brandy and liqueurs while I related the tale of my mother-in-law's desire for a larger house.

"She has an edifice complex," Black Moustache said.

I found this incredibly funny and laughed until tears ran on my cheeks. My companions floated in and out of my vision, astounding me with their fabulous conversation. I was on the cusp of great things, but felt completely tranquil. The mother of my children might be angry, but these men understood. I drank some more.

Then something happened. My euphoria collapsed. I remembered my wife, alone upstairs, and my happiness turned to guilt. My new friends sympathised. Yes, the world was unjust. Yes, the institution of marriage was fraught with danger. Yes, we were unlucky in love. After that, the evening became murky. I remember feeling ill and going to the bathroom. I also recall riding in a car. I came to myself in a booth in a café. Someone was shaking me. There were plates and cups on the table.

"Wake up," a woman's voice said. "Your friends have gone. They left you snoring with your head on the table. They said you'd pay."

Warm sun shone through the window. My hair hurt and my teeth itched. My brain pulsated against the backs of my eyes. "Where am I?" I asked.

"You're in the Rooster Grill in Gopher Grove, Saskatchewan," she answered.

"I have to get back to the Holiday Inn. How far is it?"

She laughed. "You're nowhere near. We're a blink on the highway. The Holiday Inn is in the city, over a hundred miles away."

Somewhere, in the depth of my hangover, a light bulb went on. I felt my pocket. My wallet was gone. So was my wrist watch. The only thing I had was my room key.

"They said you'd pay," the waitress repeated.

"I can't. They took my money."

She stared at me, not happy. "You don't look like a crook," she said. "You can work it off."

I gathered the cobwebs in my brain and rolled up my sleeves. The unfamiliar work didn't keep me from thinking how angry my wife would be. I dreaded going back. I'd never been in so much trouble. Her family was difficult, but I loved her and didn't relish the idea of spending the rest of my life alone. There was no doubt she would order me to leave. She'd probably already returned home to throw out my belongings and tell her mother about my treachery.

By late afternoon the bill was paid. I stood on the side of the highway and put my thumb out. The return to the city took hours; it was ten o'clock when I entered the hotel.

The bar by the lobby was empty. I felt tired and my back ached, so I charged a double to the room.

The drink made me feel worse. Perhaps she hadn't left. Maybe she was in the room waiting to kill me. I shuddered and left the bar. I had no excuse and no speech ready. There was no sound. I turned the key and opened the door.

The only light came from a desk lamp. The mother of my children was sitting in the shadows on the side of the bed. She looked up and I saw she was crying. "Studsy," she whispered. Then she stood, ran across the room and threw her arms around me.

My mouth fell open. I had expected a flying water tumbler. The words poured from her. "You scared me half to death. I thought you'd gone for good. Please don't frighten me like that. I'll never be mean to you again." She shivered and sobbed, making my shirt wet.

I couldn't believe it. She thought I'd walked out because I was sore — left everything: her, my children, my home, my job. A lump formed in my throat. I opened my mouth to tell her the truth — that I'd got drunk, that I'd been kidnapped and robbed.

"Don't cry," I said. "It's not like that. I didn't leave you. I . . . I . . . "

I opened my mouth but something made me stop: those years together, our children, her belief that I could actually just take off like the good cowboy at the end of a western movie. A tear rolled on my cheek. She'd called me Studsy, after all these years. Maybe it was better if she thought I was angry instead of stupid.

I pulled her close. "I won't leave you again," I said.

She stretched up and kissed me. "I love you, Studsy," she said.

We held hands as we walked down to the dining room. I was tired and I had a hangover, but everything felt good. Oh yes . . . that spark . . . it became an inferno!

GALLOPING FASTER *than the* WIND

One night, when I was fourteen and still believed the world was a magnificent place where everything was possible, I was awakened from a sound sleep by a stone hitting my bedroom window. The hands on my clock shone in the dark. It was one AM.

I jumped out of bed, and in the moonlight flooding our yard I saw my cousin Angela. She had long black hair and the wind was blowing it like a dark streak. The caraganas along the lane cast a shadow that hid her legs so she seemed to float in the centre of our yard. At first I thought I might be dreaming, because it had been almost two years since she'd thrown a stone at my window.

Back then, Angela enjoyed being alive so much that she couldn't sleep. She'd wake me and my sister Katie and we'd go with her to enjoy the world. We roamed the town to see what folks did at night and we swam through stars shining in Linner's Pond. We ate from people's gardens, and once we rode Mister Dixon's horses all the way to Blackjacket Lake. Her excitement always gathered us up and floated us along like geese on a river.

For a minute I thought it was old times. Then I remembered. I opened my window and put my finger to my lips. "Shhh . . . you're going to wake the folks. Hold your horses."

She trembled with impatience, making her long shadow dance on our lawn. "Call Katie," she whispered. Katie's room was next to my parent's so Angela didn't dare throw a stone at her window.

"Katie's not here. She stayed at her girlfriend's."

"Then you come, Mackie. Hurry!"

I put on jeans and a T-shirt, slid out the window and joined her on the dew-wet grass.

"Come," she said, and pulled my arm until we were in the lane behind the caraganas.

"What do you want?" I asked. "Why did you wake me at one in the morning?"

"It's an emergency. I need your help, Mackie."

I could tell by her voice, and her face in the moonlight, that she was serious. You can always tell when my cousin Angela is serious. Her voice gets real low and shakes like she's going to cry, and her lip trembles like it expects tears to fall on it.

"Will you babysit? I have to go out."

"Go out? It's one o'clock in the morning! Where are you going?"

"Not far. I'll hurry back, I promise."

"What's the emergency, Angela? Why are you being so secret?"

"There's no secret, Mackie. Braz is back. He wants to take Little Guy. His folks put him up to it." Her voice was still shaking. My cousin Angela doesn't cry, but she was close.

"You mean Braz is here? In town?"

"Yeah, he's back. I have to change his mind. Sit for me, okay?"

"Okay Angela. Where's Braz now?

"He phoned. He's on his way. I'm going out with him but I don't want him near Little Guy. Let's go, we have to hurry."

We started back to her place. "Thanks Mackie. You have to feed Little Guy if he cries and change him if he's wet. Can you do that?"

"Sure Angela, I can do that." She had enough worries. I didn't need to tell her I'd never babysat before. Usually Katie looked after Little Guy if Angela had to go out.

"Here's the key, Mackie. I locked the door so Braz can't get in. He'd steal Little Guy for sure."

Angela's room was in the basement of the oldest house on the block. There was a red convertible parked in front. Braz was behind the wheel drinking a beer and smoking a cigarette.

He stared hard at Angela. "What the hell happened to you? I've been here over twenty minutes. You locked me out." His words were slurred. It didn't take a huge brain to figure out he'd been drinking more than the beer he had in his hand.

Angela went over to the car. "Sorry Braz. I had to get Mackie to babysit."

"What do you mean babysit? You and me are meeting inside."

"No Braz. Little Guy's sleeping. You're not going to wake him up."

"I got a right to see my son." He got out of the car.

Angela crouched like she was going to tackle him if he started toward the house. Braz took a swig of beer to crank himself up.

"We gotta discuss his future, Angela. You know that. My folks want him and they can look after him. He doesn't need to grow up in this shit." He waved at the house and flipped his cigarette into the street. It lay there glowing in the dirt.

He banged his fist on the side of the car. "I got a right to see my kid," he shouted. He stepped toward Angela and I tensed up. He looked like he was going to hit her.

An upstairs window opened across the street and someone yelled for us to shut up. Braz grinned and dropped his hands to his sides. "Come on, Angela. I want to see him. He is my kid, ain't he?"

"Yes and no, Braz. You weren't interested until your folks got interested. It's not a good idea. It's late and Little Guy is sleeping."

A sly look came over his face. "You might as well give it up Angela. We're going to get him anyway."

"No, you're not! You don't love him. Your folks only want him because of all the lies you told about me being unfit." Angela was mad. You can always tell when my cousin Angela is mad. Her lip curls and her arms come up like she's going to start swinging.

She clenched her teeth and swallowed to control her temper. "That's enough, Braz. Let's go now. We can discuss it in the car."

He lit another cigarette and left it dangling from his lip. In the dim light, with his collar turned up, he looked like a surly rock singer. "It don't matter, Angela. I'll see him lots when my folks get him."

He made an exaggerated show of opening the passenger door. She slid in and looked at me. "I won't be long Mackie."

"Yeah, she won't be long, Mackie," he mimicked.

He got behind the wheel, started the car and floored it. The tires squealed as he sped down the street and turned the corner.

I went into Angela's room and found the light switch. The place was so small I couldn't turn around without bumping my nose. Circus posters hung on the walls and clothes were scattered everywhere – on the chair, on the table. There was even frilly stuff on the radiator. She slept on the sofa and it hadn't been made up.

Her little boy was standing in his crib. I think I scared him, because he started to howl like a lonely coyote. I told him, "Don't cry," but he just put his head back and hollered. I didn't know what to do so I picked him up and jiggled him. He quit being afraid and got mad. His face turned red. His mouth, nose and eyes started running and every time he let out a beller he sprayed me. I thought if I fed him he might quiet down. He was chubby and heavy, so I set him back in the crib and let him wail.

🦋 🦋

Maybe I should explain about my cousin Angela. She's only sixteen but she has a ten-month old baby she calls Little Guy, though his real name is Reginald Maxwell Livingstone the Third. She named him that so he'd have a head start in life. She and Little Guy have lived in the basement room since her folks kicked her out for making them feel ashamed. She pays the rent by waiting tables down at Louie's Cafe. It's a good job in one way. Louie lets Angela bring Little Guy to work. It's not a good job in another way. Drunks come in after the beer parlour closes and make remarks about Angela being an unwed mother. They call her the town bicycle. She gets mad but that makes them worse. Things even out, though — some of them get a lot more in their hamburgers than what they order.

🦋 🦋

I found milk in the fridge and cookies in the cupboard, but when I tried to feed Little Guy, he locked his jaws. I reckoned I'd have to trick him, so I crumbled a cookie into a glass of milk, and stirred it until there weren't any chunks left. It didn't work. He kept his mouth closed and most of it spilled in his crib.

I thought maybe the milk was too cold so I poured it into an electric kettle and plugged it in. In a couple of minutes, he was quiet and guzzling out of the glass although lots of milk dribbled down his front. He wanted more so I dissolved the rest of the cookies.

〜 〜

Braz left town when Angela got pregnant. He's about four years older than she is. He told the guys in the poolroom he didn't bargain on any baby when he started putting the meat to Angela. He told her he wasn't ready to be no daddy. He said if she was dumb enough to get knocked up, then it was her problem. Once he left, we thought we'd never see him again. Me and Katie figured Angela was better off without him.

Most folks don't have much to do with her because she's got a bad reputation. The old people think she's a sinner and the ones she went to school with seem embarrassed around her. About the only people she talks to, apart from drunks that come in the cafe, are me and my sister Katie. Our folks are the only ones who don't think what she's got will rub off.

Her parents weren't easy on her either. Her old man can be rougher than a sandpaper diaper. They're mean to her and they give her knots in her stomach when they try to get between her and Little Guy.

〜 〜

Little Guy stuck out his lower lip and I could see a whimper coming. She'd said to change him. I searched high and low but couldn't find anything that looked like a diaper. The dish towel was dirty. Finally, I had an idea. I took off his wet stuff and pinned him up in a pillowcase. It slid off when he stood up.

I found scissors in a drawer and cut the corners out of the pillowcase. I put his legs through the corners and pulled it up over him. I cut holes for his arms and then I tied the top over his head so he was standing in a bag. He seemed scared so I cut a hole for his face to look out. He quit crying right away and we started to get along just fine.

≈ ≈

I don't remember when the three of us weren't together. We used to pretend we were grown up. Katie would be a famous movie star and I was always a ball player. Angela wanted to be a trick rider in the circus. She said she wanted to wear a red outfit with sparkling sequins. Then she would ride out of a fog made by a machine and gallop through the arena standing on the back of a white horse, hair streaming behind her. The audience would clap and yell. Then she'd stand on her hands, and the horse would gallop faster than the wind, around and around, until everyone was dizzy from watching her.

We told her she'd probably get killed, but she said it wouldn't matter, because once you'd galloped faster than the wind, you could never feel the same again. That was my cousin Angela. Her dreams weren't everyday ones, like being a movie star or a ball player. Her dreams had details.

What amazed us is, Angela worked on her dream. She got permission from Mr. Dixon to ride one of his horses, and she practised until she could stand on its back while it trotted around the corral. When she fell off, she got up and started over. She scared Katie and me, because she kept going no matter how much she hurt herself. Mr. Dixon said he'd never seen anybody stay with something the way Angela did. He said, with her attitude, she'd be riding one day – either on a horse or in a wheelchair.

≈ ≈

Little Guy stood in his crib and I sat in a chair while we carried on a conversation. He liked to talk and I didn't mind listening. Most of his words didn't come out in English but it didn't make any difference. We had one of those conversations where it doesn't matter what you say. What's important is talking.

His dark curly hair stuck out around the hole in the pillowcase. He had a small nose and fat cheeks. When he grinned, I could see some teeth. He was still grinning when I nodded off.

꙰   ꙰

One night Angela, Katie and me were walking home from a movie. Braz picked us up in his daddy's car. That's when it started. Angela fell head-over-heels. He was a big deal in town, good looking and his family had money. All the girls were after him. I think maybe he was one of her dreams, like being a trick rider.

After that we didn't see much of Angela. She wasn't interested in the same things anymore. When we did run into her, all she talked about was "Braz this and Braz that." Me and Katie agreed it was kind of sickening.

Whispers flew return trips over backyard fences when she got pregnant. Mr. and Mrs. Brazeau blamed her for Braz leaving town. To hear them tell it, Angela seduced him and wrecked his entire life. They did everything they could to make her miserable and get her fired from Louie's. They'd also been doing everything they could to take Little Guy away from her.

꙰   ꙰

Morning rolled around. Little Guy and I were both asleep when Angela came running in. She pulled a suitcase from behind the sofa.

"Quick, Mackie. Help me pack. Me and Little Guy are leaving town."

She noticed the pillow on him. "My God, why have you got him dressed like an elf in a Christmas concert?"

"I couldn't find any diapers. What happened, Angela? Why are you leaving?"

"'To get away. The Brazeaus want to take Little Guy, and they can do it, because I'm under age. Braz does whatever his parents tell him. The diapers are on the floor under the crib.'" She walked around the room gathering up her clothes.

"But where are you going, Angela? How are you going? You don't have a car."

She tossed the clothes in the suitcase and gave me a grin. "Oh yes I do. Hand me the diapers, Mackie. I got a big red convertible sitting right outside."

I reached under the crib and bumped my head. Little Guy woke up and started to cry. "You got Braz's car! I don't get it, Angela. How come he's letting you drive his car?"

She picked up Little Guy, hugged him, undid the pillowcase and spread a diaper on the table. "Who said he's letting me drive it?" Her grin got bigger.

"You took it! Where's Braz? Doesn't he know you've got it?"

Little Guy stopped crying. "Sure he does, Mackie. But he's got a ten mile hike out of the bush before he can report it. By that time, I'll be long gone. Me and Little Guy will be on our way to a new life. Here, hold him for a minute, please."

I couldn't believe it! She stole his car! It couldn't have been easy. "How'd you get it, Angela? I know he didn't hand you the keys."

She laughed, pulled a poster off the wall, folded it, and put it in the suitcase. "He was drinking beer and we drove back in the bush. He wouldn't talk about Little Guy. His real reason for wanting me to come out was to play backseat basketball. I kept blocking him until he needed time out for a whiz. Then I drove away."

She took Little Guy and went outside. I crammed everything down, closed the suitcase, and followed her. She put Little Guy in the passenger seat and gave me a hug.

"What are you going to do, Angela? I know you don't have much money."

She slipped behind the wheel. "I don't know," she said. "I just know I can't stay. Maybe me and Little Guy will join the circus." Her eyes glistened. She pushed her jaw out and set her lips tight so they didn't tremble. "Goodbye, Mackie," she said.

Dawn was just a few minutes away—the time of day when the magnificence of the world becomes clear and everything is possible. I watched her drive away. She looked determined. You can always tell when my cousin Angela is determined. She doesn't slow down and she never looks back. She stepped on the gas and the car jumped ahead. The wind had picked up and Angela's long hair blew straight out behind her.

SEASONS *in a* PARKED CAR

Wisps of summer fog moved across the prairie, covering and uncovering the lights in Tuckahoe. The dark shape of the town appeared and disappeared with the lights. Frogs croaked on the river flats. The fog made the air musty and the smell of new-mown hay invaded their nostrils. Elvis sang "Love Me Tender" and the green glow from the car radio reflected on the girl's face.

"Cigarette?" He pulled a package of Players from his shirt pocket. She took one. He hummed along with the radio and held out the glowing end of the lighter. She lit the cigarette and exhaled toward the open window.

"It looks like a cardboard cut-out," she said.

"What?"

"The town. It looks like it only has two dimensions."

"Oh, yeah," he said. "Two dimensions."

He dragged on his cigarette and let the smoke trickle from his nose.

"The frogs sound like crickets," she said.

"Oh, yeah," he said. "Crickets."

"There's a flying saucer," she said.

"Oh, yeah," he said. "A flying saucer."

He set his cigarette in the ashtray, extracted a comb from his back pocket, leaned forward and combed his dark hair in the rear-view mirror. She watched him tease his ducktail into place.

"You don't listen to me," she said.

"Sure I do. You just said I don't listen to you."

"Do you want to go to the dance?" she asked.

"Not now."

"I'm afraid," she said.

"Oh." He poked the soft dice hanging from the mirror. They swung in the ribbon of smoke curling up from the ashtray.

"Did you hear me? I said I'm afraid."

He leaned forward, put the comb away and retrieved his cigarette.

"Why?" he asked.

She didn't answer. He inhaled and waited.

"Is something wrong?" he asked.

She edged away and leaned against the car door. "You said you would."

"What?"

"You said you'd be careful." She stubbed her cigarette in the ashtray and pushed her hands into her jacket pockets.

"I told you, I left them at home."

"I know. You said you'd stop in time."

He threw his cigarette out the window and turned up the radio. "All Shook Up" drowned out the frogs on the river flats.

"I meant to, Ellie. I'm sorry." He fished in his jacket pocket. "Gum?" he asked.

"We should have waited," she said.

"I waited almost a year."

"A little longer…until I finished school."

"That's another year. What's school got to do with it?"

"Nothing I guess. It seems like we spent the whole year in your car. I couldn't relax."

"I said I was sorry." He put the gum back in his jacket.

Her left hand escaped her pocket and set her fingers tapping on the car seat. She retrieved her fingers and pressed them into her lap. "What if something happens?"

"It won't. There's only one chance in ten."

"Only what?"

"The odds are one in ten. I read it somewhere. Nothing will happen."

"Oh," she said. "But what if it does?"

"Don't worry about it," he said.

She slid across the seat and put her hand on his arm. "Write to me while you're at university?" she said.

"Every day." He laughed.

"I'm glad you love me," she said. "It makes me feel better."

He reached out and turned the key. Her hand dropped from his arm. The motor purred and the muffler growled. He guided the car in a circle and started down the hill into town.

🙟 🙜

Fall moonlight reflected on the hood of the blue Pontiac. Lights from the town formed coloured streaks on the damp windshield. A flock of geese gaggled on the river. Grain dust from afternoon harvesting seeped into the car and tickled their nostrils. Elvis sang "I Got Stung" and the green glow from the radio illuminated a tight smile on the girl's face.

She exhaled and her breath misted the streaks. He sat straight and gripped the steering wheel. She stared through the colours in the window.

"They look like rainbows," she said.

"What?"

"The streaks on the window. They look like rainbows."

"Oh yeah," he said. "Rainbows."

"You didn't write," she said.

"I was busy. I forgot."

"I quit school," she said.

"So I heard."

"We beat the odds," she said.

"Damn, Ellie, I didn't think it would happen." His fingers tapped the keys hanging from the ignition and his knee danced nervously under the dash.

"What did he say?" he asked.

"Who?"

"The doctor. What did he say?"

"Everything's fine. It's going along just as it should."

"Yeah, just as it should. Have you told anybody?" he asked.

"No, I haven't."

"Good. What do we do now?"

"What do you think we should do?"

He lit a cigarette and turned the dial on the radio. Elvis sang "I Feel So Bad".

"We have to do something," he said. "We don't want people to find out." His fingers jangled the keys as he picked up the rhythm from the song.

"What do you suggest?"

"There are ways to deal with these situations. I've read about it."

"In Tuckahoe?" she asked.

"In a bigger place. It doesn't take long and it's not dangerous."

"Not dangerous for you," she said.

He tapped his cigarette on the gear shift and the ash fell to the floor. "I could ask around," he said.

She turned and looked at him. "Is that all?"

"I don't know what else."

"Never mind. I'm going to have it."

"Yeah," he said. "Have it."

He hesitated and the words came slow, swelling into each other the way mould grows on forgotten leftovers. "Have it. Then put it up for adoption. Come to the city. I'll get a job until you give it up. My folks will think I'm still going to classes. No one will know."

"No," she said. "I'm going to keep it."

He pushed his fist into the seat. "I guess we could get married. But we can't tell anybody. My dad wouldn't understand. I have to finish university."

She stared at him. "Yes, we could get married, but I don't care who knows as long as you love me."

He shrugged and twisted the key. The motor purred and the muffler growled. He stepped on the gas. The car spun around and started down the hill into town.

❧ ❧

A carpet of snow covered the hill. Beams from street lights stretched into elongated spears and pointed to the car, parked and idling above the town. The heater poured warm air into the front seat. Water gurgled as it ducked under the ice near the river bank. Wood smoke from kitchen stoves crept up the hill and was pulled into the car. It chafed their nostrils. Elvis sang "Wear My Ring Around Your Neck", and the girl's face looked strained in the green glow from the radio.

He threw back his head and closed his eyes. She fidgeted on the seat and sighed through her carefully composed face.

"They look like golden paths," she said.

"What?"

"The lights from town. They look like golden paths coming up the hill."

"Oh yeah," he said. "Golden paths."

"I'm waiting tables at Louie's," she said.

"I heard."

"Time's passing," she said.

He leaned over until his forehead rested on the steering wheel. "There's a problem. No one's supposed to know."

"What?"

He whispered to the horn in the centre of the steering wheel. "My friends, the town, Ellie. It's just a matter of time until Dad finds out."

"I can't hide it, you know."

"Why do people have to know it was me?"

"It's obvious. We've been going out for over a year."

"Well, I can't now."

"Can't what?"

"Get married. I can't get married now."

She didn't move. "Why not?"

"My dad. Remember he threatened to throw me out if I kept seeing you."

"That was before," she said.

"It'll be worse now."

"So what do we do?" she asked.

"You can do what you want, but I can't marry you. School is my only chance. He hates everything else I've done."

He pushed a button on the radio. Static came from the speaker. Through the static Elvis sang "It's Now or Never".

She gave him a thousand-mile stare and reached for his hand. "Don't you love me?" she asked.

He started to speak. Then he pressed his lips together and pulled the gear shift. The motor purred and the muffler growled. The car fish-tailed in the snow and they started down the hill into the town.

❧ ❧

A shadow moved over the prairie and vanished into the run-off valley on the side of the hill. Poplar leaves, laundered by spring rain, shone in the light of a disappearing sun. The conversations of migrating ducks cluttered the air over the river flats. The smell of washed landscape filled their nostrils. The sound of Elvis singing "A Fool Such As I" floated out through an open window. The baby slept, serene in the green glow from the radio.

She smoothed the blanket and lightly ran her hand over the tiny head.

"They look like spinning silver coins," she said.

"What?"

"The leaves," she said. "They look like spinning silver coins."

"Oh yeah," he said. "Silver coins."

She lifted the blanket. "What do you think of your son? Isn't he cute?"

"Oh yeah," he said. "Cute."

There was silence.

"Your son," she said. "What do you think of him?"

"Cigarette?" he asked.

"Put them away. You can't smoke around the baby."

Again silence. "When did you get back? Why did you call after all this time?" she asked.

"I had to, Ellie. My dad says I need to take responsibility for my actions."

The baby murmured in its sleep.

"Responsibility?" she asked.

"Dad says his grandson is not going to be a bastard. We have to get married."

"Get married!" She gripped the blanket with both hands. "It's what I wanted."

"Good," he said. "Let's do it . . . small . . . just my family. We don't want to advertise."

Her fingers twisted the blanket. "No . . . we don't want to advertise," she said.

"I'll set things up. We can get it over with and get back to normal . . . the way it was."

"Yes," she said. "The way it was."

He looked at her. "You're repeating everything I say. You're not listening to me."

"Repeating," she said. "Not listening."

"No matter," he said. "It's settled."

"How was it?" she asked.

"What?"

"You said 'the way it was'. How was it?"

He turned the key. The motor purred and the muffler growled.

She opened the door and stepped out, carrying the baby. Elvis' voice singing "Hard Headed Woman" exited the open door.

"What are you doing?" he asked. "Where are you going?"

Her voice was low, barely audible. "I don't love you," she said.

Then, staring straight ahead, Ellie turned and started down the hill into the town.

EMILE SLIDEBOTTLE *is a* PIECE *of* WORK

Molly Colestead had been a widow for twenty-two years. She was a gentle lady, small in stature and large in good will. Folks in Tuckahoe adored her. A volunteer's volunteer, she worked at the school, helped with the Christmas concert, collected for the Red Cross and babysat for neighbours. The small cottage where she lived alone was at the crossroads of every worthwhile activity in town.

She had been a war bride from England and her roots ran deep. On Sunday mornings her white hair curled over the collar of her black coat as she trudged two blocks to attend services at the Anglican Church. She lived a quiet life, tended her garden and every year her chokecherry muffins and rhubarb pie won ribbons at Tuckahoe's summer fair.

Her next door neighbour was Anetskya Rezansoff, also a widow and well-respected. Folks called her Annie. Her girth was the size of her heart and that was huge. She also helped at community events and won prizes at the fair. Between Annie and Molly, they took home all the ribbons. Competition between them was amiable. Though one was born in England and the other in the Ukraine, they had side-stepped all the cultural stereotypes and become friends.

Folks mistook one for the other, although they looked nothing alike. The resemblance was in the shape of their generosity and in the energy they expended on the style of their lives.

Through the years they had survived floods, droughts and husbands. Each had captained a fatherless family and, periodically, launched a new adult into the larger world. They were alone now with only memories of family calamities. Measles, chicken pox, broken bones and the attendant worries had been passed to the next generation.

Strong convictions gave each an inner strength, supplemented by a coalition of purpose. They shared everything: loneliness, memories of youth, new recipes for borscht, a joint-venture garden and a tall maple tree, anchored in one yard with branches spread over the other. Annie's garden shed overlapped into Molly Colestead's yard. Measurement by the town office showed an enclosed veranda on the side of Molly's cottage encroached onto Annie's property by exactly two feet. None of this caused concern. Boundaries were unimportant. The ladies got along fine. Each drew strength from the other, and the fabric of their friendship had never frayed.

Molly summed it up one evening while they shared a glass of rhubarb wine. "The next best thing to having a lively man in your house is having a neighbour who's your best friend."

Annie raised her glass. "I drink to that," she said. "But, maybe lively man not stay in house, just in bed . . . one . . . two times a week "

Tears were on both their cheeks by the time they quit laughing, and the bottle was empty when Molly left for home.

❧ ☙

Like many episodes in the human story, it started with the weather. Though it was summer, the sky blew dark for days. Rain fell and almost froze in the cold wind. Folks stayed inside and tried to wait it out.

Mr. Reginald Slidebottle, who lived across the street from the two ladies, was no exception. He hovered near his kitchen stove with only Strumpet, his ancient half-blind cat, for company. Strumpet provided little in the way of conversation, and after three days of confinement, Reginald ventured two blocks to Louie's Café for coffee and human companionship.

Unfortunately the companionship happened to be burly Nels Larson, who was nursing a nasty head cold. Sometime during their discussion of the weather and other world affairs, a malicious virus leapt from Nels to Reginald and settled down to incubate. Reginald came down with a cold. He was old and so was his immune system. After steadily increasing sniffles, he started to cough. The virus had hit the jackpot. Reginald succumbed and went to meet his maker, still sniffling.

The ladies were dutifully saddened at his passing. They attended his funeral and, as token of their respect, watered flowers and trimmed the grass in his yard. They also fed Strumpet, who daily slunk along Reginald's back fence, tail in the air, trying to re-enact a distant memory of enticement. No male cats came and Strumpet usually retired to the front step to lie in the sun and dream of past seduction.

"That cat don't know she too old," Annie said. "She like me. Only good for memory, now."

One day Molly heard music coming from Reginald's house. She noticed curtains open and lights on. Thinking someone was trespassing, she crossed the street and knocked on the door. It was opened by a strange apparition. "Yes Ma'am, what can I do for you?" the apparition squeaked.

"I live across the street. Have you purchased Mr. Slidebottle's house?" Molly asked.

The apparition adjusted his hair, which didn't appear to be anchored to his head. He smiled and his lips gave way to large protruding teeth that had more gaps than a truant's alibi.

"Why, no. My name is Emile Slidebottle. I've just come from Stoneboat Creek. Reginald was my uncle. He left this house to me. I'm planning to live here." One after the other his eyes rolled into place beneath the single raised brow that ran the width of his lower forehead.

Strumpet meowed loudly and began to march back and forth, rubbing herself wantonly against Emile's leg. Molly looked down and felt a sensation she vaguely recognised, but couldn't identify, like the memory of perfume worn by a grade one teacher.

"Emile Slidebottle is a piece of work," she later confided to Annie.

Little did she know. From his first teacher to his last warden, Emile had always exceeded everyone's capacity to be under-whelmed. He was the kind of man who slips along his allotted span, the path lubricated by the work of others. It was his proud boast that effort was unnecessary.

"I've never read a complete newspaper, magazine, or book," he once bragged to his parole officer. "Somebody always tells me anything I have to know and gives me anything I need. All I have to do is ask."

Emile wasn't completely true to his credo and he wasn't lazy all the time. He was a passionate believer in short cuts, however. So when asking didn't do the trick, he helped things along by taking what he required, often from lonely widows. Growth was as sparse inside his head as on the outside, so he frequently got caught. A fair portion of his life had been spent as a guest of local authorities.

When he learned he'd inherited a house in Tuckahoe, he almost ignored his good fortune. Not entirely incorrect, he surmised to his cellmate, "If Tuckahoe ain't the end of the world, it's probably within pissin' distance on a windy day." And if that were the case, what chance would there be for a man with his ability to exercise his well-honed talents?

But destiny is fickle, and Emile's coming-out project, a sixty-year-old widow from Stoneboat Creek, turned out to be the sister of the local policeman. It became necessary for him to take a hasty holiday. Reginald's house seemed as good a place as any for an enterprising man to take a breather from the rigours of earning his daily bread.

When he learned the circumstance of the two ladies, and of the dearth of husband material in Tuckahoe, his heart did a pirouette and danced a jig across his ego. A remote town, his own house, two widows with no nearby relatives, a part-time town cop — God had sent him a new project. Maybe it was he, and not his uncle, who'd died and gone to heaven. He flashed his few large teeth, wet down his eyebrow and adjusted his hair to a more rakish angle in the bathroom mirror.

When it came to projects Emile was not a passive man. He approached each one with the intensity of a boy staring at ads for ladies' underwear. Like all good campaigns, his started slowly. He took to visiting both ladies, but only one at a time, and only when the other was away. Gradually, he increased the frequency and decreased the secrecy.

He dreamt up questions about life in Tuckahoe. Where was the best place to buy groceries? How far did he have to drive to do his banking? Who should he call to fix the plumbing? Where was the best place for a lonely and hungry bachelor to eat?

The ladies were flattered. It wasn't often someone asked their advice . . . and then took it. Emile didn't discriminate. He visited both equally, usually at meal times.

They outdid themselves. Both were talented and both had spent years vying for ribbons at the fair. For the first time each saw herself in real competition with the other. Not only did Emile dine sumptuously at least twice a day, he found himself inundated with chocolate cakes, fresh pies, perogies, cookies, cabbage rolls and cinnamon buns. He swallowed the attention the way a pig sucks up slop. Both he and his fridge were stuffed most of the time.

Emile's early years had left their influence. He'd been born at home and was still in diapers when his parents got religion and gave him away so they could become travelling evangelists. His new parents were itinerant marriage counsellors who criss-crossed the country in a small trailer. They stopped in little towns where his dad found clients in the beer parlour and his mom conducted counselling sessions in the trailer.

As he grew older, Emile was told to go outside during the sessions. One day, while playing under the trailer, he found a salamander. He made a box for it and gave it dead flies to eat. He named it Lila, after a friend of his mother's. He cared for Lila and the caring blossomed into love. Unfortunately, one day, Lila crawled beneath the sheets of his mother's bed and was crushed to death during one of her counselling sessions. Emile was devastated. It was years before he could look at a dead fly without sadness brimming in his soul.

So Strumpet filled a long-suppressed need. He fed her and she slept on his feet. He discovered emotions he hadn't felt since before Lila was crushed. He became devoted to the old cat and pandered to its every need.

In the meantime it became apparent that the fabric of Annie and Molly's friendship had two sides. On the top strong stitching held the pattern of their daily lives in place. On the bottom the pattern was less distinct. Nestled below the fabric, as drowsy as two bears in spring, a pair of libidos were waking up after a long hibernation.

Gradually the ladies found less time to share a coffee or glass of rhubarb wine. When they met they passed quickly, commenting only on the weather. As a subject of conversation, Emile was off-limits. Tight-lipped, they played his game with an intensity rarely seen outside professional sporting events.

One night, Annie awoke to a call from nature and padded through her house in the dark. Moonlight flooded her yard, and as she passed her kitchen window, she noticed a figure hard at work in the back garden. She watched Molly move cucumber, zucchini and pumpkin vines so the fruit was all repositioned in the Colestead yard. Then she picked tomatoes, dug potatoes and cut cauliflower. All were clearly on Annie's side.

"That no-good hussy stealing my vegetables," she said out loud. "I fix her."

The next Sunday, when Molly returned from church, she found the limbs that had provided shade in her yard severed from the maple. Only the branches that covered Annie's yard still protruded from the tree. *This is going too far*, Molly thought. *It's time we made up.*

But reconciliation is difficult, like jumping from a moving train — a simple task when the train is pulling from the station, but terrifying when the speed is up. It's easier and safer to stay aboard . . . and that's exactly what they did. Before Molly could act, Annie upped the ante again.

The next morning Molly awoke at 5:00 am to the banshee-like howl of an old tomcat. Unfortunately the serenade had given Strumpet a headache and so, exercising the prerogative of all females, she refused to respond. Undeterred, the tomcat increased the volume. Sleep was not an option, so Molly got up to cook an early breakfast. She glanced out the window and saw Emile, carrying his hair in his hand, hurriedly crossing the street from Annie's house. He was also carrying his shoes and trying to zip up his fly. Smoke began to rise from her toaster but she waited until the toast was charcoal before she pulled the plug.

That afternoon, Annie returned from a meeting of the Tuckahoe Busy Beavers Homemakers' Club. It was raining and she noticed tractor tracks leading off the street into her yard. Her garden shed had been neatly pulled back onto her property.

While inspecting for damage she saw Emile, in a new suit, crossing the street and carrying a bottle of wine. Molly's door opened and he slipped inside. Jealousy slammed into Annie and flared like gas on a bonfire. She knelt, faint from the heat of it.

She pondered her options. There weren't many. Apart from homicide, it was hard to come up with ideas. She felt torn inside but knew that whatever she did had to make Molly lay off Emile for good.

Her opportunity soon came.

Molly left for her annual stint as chaperone at a weekend Brownie camp. She was nervous about leaving, but had little choice. The Brownies were short of volunteers.

The weather was balmy and the camp a big success. Molly returned, high spirits tempered by trepidation. As she walked down her street she breathed a sigh of relief. Everything looked okay . . . until she turned into her yard. From the tip of the roof to the foundation, the interior of her enclosed veranda was exposed. Exactly two feet had been neatly sawed away, and the entire west wall was lying in Annie's yard. Family pictures were still on the wall, askew and face up in the afternoon sun.

Rage swept over her. "Killing's too good for that Jezebel," she snapped out loud. "I've got to do something else." But what? Escalation was hurting them both. Gradually anger gave way. A sly look appeared on her face. She resolved to disarm Annie with kindness before exacting her revenge.

In the morning she appeared on Annie's doorstep, a freshly baked pie in her hands, and an apology on her lips. "I came because this whole thing has gone too far," she explained. "We've been friends for years and we've let circumstances drive us apart. It's time we made up."

At first, Annie was nervous and suspicious, but she missed their easy friendship. She accepted the pie, invited Molly inside and put on a pot of coffee. The conflict had been tearing her apart and she felt a surge of relief. Her face and heart opened. "Oh, thank heavens. I've been feel bad. I didn't know how to tell you."

"Tell me what?" Molly demanded. Her stomach tightened. What else had Annie done?

"About Emile and me. We getting married," Annie said. She beamed and the loneliness came pouring out. "Lots of nights I cry myself to sleep remembering family, remembering when I had love of good man," she confessed. "I have to marry him, Molly. He ask me. There's not many years left. I want to be happy. He is first to ask. Maybe no more chance."

At first the devil inside Molly grinned at Annie's confession. A dalliance was one thing, but Emile Slidebottle was not husband material. Annie would get what she deserved.

Then selfishness pushed the devil aside. What about me? she asked herself. I'll be all alone while they snuggle beneath the blankets. It's not fair.

Finally her conscience took over. The bond of friendship proved stronger than the string that ties jealousy and revenge together. Her stomach, already tight, shrivelled in fear for her friend. *I have to stop this*, she thought. *But how? There was no way to do it without appearing jealous. Objecting without a valid reason would only strengthen Annie's resolve.*

Aloud she said, "Yes, you deserve it, dear. I'm pleased as peanut brittle for you."

She returned home despondent. In low spirits, she dialed the hardware store and ordered a canvas cover for the west side of her veranda.

Molly quit seeing Emile, which suited him fine. Although he was a little short in some departments, he did have a sixth sense about these matters. He had not made his decision on a whim. Careful sleuthing had helped. Annie had considerably more money than Molly, so there really was no decision. *She's as well-heeled as a six-foot stripper*, Emile thought gleefully. He'd popped the question that evening.

Time wound down to the wedding. Molly still had no idea how to keep Annie from marrying Emile. She needed a plan, and for that she needed information. Emile had told her he once lived in Stoneboat Creek. Molly had a friend there. She screwed up her nerve, started her ancient Ford and weaved her way slowly to the larger town. If anyone would know about Emile's past it would be her friend, a sixty year-old widow privy to all kinds of information. The widow's brother was the only policeman in Stoneboat Creek.

❧ ❧

With only days to go the two ladies cooked and baked like fiends. Annie was footing the bill, so Emile decided it would be a gala affair. The entire population of Tuckahoe was invited. An out-of-town band was hired. Annie strung her future with high expectations, and Emile's backyard with coloured crepe.

The sun came up brilliant on the big day. Molly was putting the finishing touches on a large wedding cake when there was a frantic knock on her door. She opened it to find Emile hopping up and down on her doorstep. He was partly dressed, white shirt half on, pants unbuttoned and hair nowhere in sight. He was breathing fast and his eyes vibrated beneath an opaque glaze. "Have you seen Strumpet?" he shouted.

Molly looked at him. "Strumpet? Well . . . let's see. I saw her yesterday."

"No! No! I mean this morning. Have you seen Strumpet this morning? She's gone . . . Missing."

"Missing? Well, I'm sure cats wander off all the time. She'll be back when she gets hungry."

Emile waved his arms, and Molly saw his hair in his hand. "No! No! She never leaves. She's not around the house. I've looked everywhere. She's missing, I tell you. Have you seen her?" His eyes rolled in separate directions under the lone brow.

"No, I'm sorry; I haven't . . . wait . . . just a minute . . . there is something. You should talk to Annie. She said something yesterday about getting rid of Strumpet for the wedding, something about not wanting a dirty old cat jumping on guests."

Emile stopped in mid-hop. His hand shook as he waved his hair under Molly's nose. "What do you mean, getting rid of her? What did she say? What did she do?" he screamed.

"I don't know, exactly. She said she didn't think she could live in the same house with Strumpet and she'd have to get rid of her before the wedding. She said the cat had to go," Molly replied.

Emile hopped up and down again. "Had to go! Had to go! She never told me. What's she done with my cat?"

Molly smiled. "I really can't say. You're going to have to take it up with her." She spoke to Emile's back. He was halfway to Annie's house, running on bare feet. Her smile widened as she licked icing off her fingers and went back inside.

She had finished the cake and was ironing her best dress when Annie came running through the back door. She was crying.

"Oh, Molly . . . Molly," she said. "I don't know what to do. Emile called off wedding. He said I do bad things to cat. I haven't seen cat. I don't hurt cat. I like cat. He say I kill cat. Then he say no wedding. Why he say that? Where is cat? What is happen?" She was sobbing.

"Oh, you poor dear," Molly said. "Come in. Sit down. Let me fix you a cup of tea while we talk."

🖋 🖋

Later, Molly fashioned a sign and put it on Emile's gate. It read, "WEDDING CANCELLED DUE TO LOST CAT. IF FOUND PLEASE CONTACT MR. E. SLIDEBOTTLE". Then she backed the Ford out of her garage, stopped for Annie, and talking with both hands inched her way out of town. Emile didn't see them go. He was in an alley three blocks away, calling for Strumpet.

On her previous trip to Stoneboat Creek, Molly had learned all she needed. The policeman's sister confided Emile's history. It became clear; Annie was Emile Slidebottle's new project. This increased Molly's dilemma. Emile wasn't just undesirable — Annie's pocketbook was in as much jeopardy as her happiness.

But she had the same problem: how to warn Annie without sounding bitter as a sour grape? She needed credibility. "I want you to meet a friend of mine," she said, as they headed toward Stoneboat Creek. Annie was too distraught to disagree.

The friend pulled no punches. Emile Slidebottle was laid bare, gutted, sliced and neatly diced. "I was going to marry him," she said. "Until my brother found out he's made a career of bedding and wedding lonely widows. You're lucky he called it off. You know he's still wanted, don't you?"

"No I didn't. I thought he'd done his time," Molly said.

"Oh no, he's wanted. All kinds of things came to light after he disappeared. They've got enough to put him away for three lifetimes. He's been involved in fraud, impersonation, passing bad cheques and bigamy. Police in a dozen towns are looking for him."

It was an impressive list. Annie shivered as she listened.

"Listen, please don't tell your brother. Emile's not dangerous, and I have an idea . . . " Molly said.

On the way back to Tuckahoe, they discussed everything. It was heartbreaking for Annie, but she was a practical lady. She clearly saw the pickle she'd almost bit into. She didn't doubt Molly. Emile Slidebottle had as much character as a bag full of mouldy toadstools.

That evening they visited Emile. He was subdued. "I don't understand," he said. "It's like she's disappeared off the face of the earth."

He looked at Annie. "You're sure you didn't do anything to her?" he asked.

"No, I didn't," Annie said. "Forget cat and listen." The tone in her voice penetrated. Emile's eyeballs clicked into place and he came to attention.

In quiet voices they told him what they knew. "But, we won't tell police," Annie said. "You help us and promise not to run away. You start by fix Molly's veranda."

"We'll think of other things," Molly added. "We're good teachers. I'm sure you can learn."

Emile wasn't happy, but he agreed. "My cat," he said pitifully. "I miss my cat."

"Don't worry," Molly said. "She's safe and well-fed in my basement. I'll give her back to you. I just borrowed her to get the wedding cancelled."

⊗ ⊗

Everything worked as planned. Emile became a moderately good cook and learned to grow a garden. On Sundays he drove the ladies to church, and after some practice was able to make a reasonable rhubarb wine. Other tasks were added to his unwritten job description. Life took on a familiar hue. Once again the ladies shared everything. A periodic summons to the appropriate house, with an order to bring his toothbrush and pyjamas, kept Emile tethered to the neighbourhood better than any leash.

Molly released Strumpet from her basement. The brief confinement must have allowed the old cat to review her courtship strategy. The very next day she returned home with a new boyfriend, an old tomcat she soon discarded in favour of a younger paramour. For Strumpet life became easy. When not patrolling her domain, she slept without dreams in the afternoon sun.

The Dancing Air Distorts

In summer, heat shimmers to the edge of the prairie. The sun bakes grass brown, and sloughs dry to cracked pavement. Buffalo once foraged here. Now gophers hide and dragonflies fold scorched wings. A road snakes around the sloughs and fades into the heat. You can see through the dancing air, but it distorts so things aren't always what they seem.

After the buffalo, a town straddled the road like a scab covers a wound. Seafoot's Store sat in the town. Its sign was in Chinese; only the owners could read it. At Seafoot's you could purchase supplies and whiskey. If you climbed the covered stairs at the back, you could lose your money at poker or buy time with Seafoot's wife. She had small breasts and bad breath. They called the town Tuckahoe.

☞　☜

The land was droning the day Fay McHale's wagon rolled out of its own dust. Another wagon followed, driven by a cowboy. They pulled to a stop in front of Seafoot's.

"Water the horses," she told the cowboy. "I'll order what we need." She jumped down and headed for the store.

She wore a man's black wool coat and denim trousers. A wide brimmed hat with a hole in the side covered her head. A few strands of blond hair had escaped through the hole. Laced calfskin boots stirred up dust as she walked. She was slender under the open coat and her movements were graceful. Even covered in dirt, she was the best-looking woman ever to set foot in Tuckahoe. She paused in front of the leering men who spent their days holding up Seafoot's walls. Her blue eyes, cold as December rain, took in everything.

"I'm Mrs. McHale," she said. "And this here's my hired help, Tom. We're going to be building down by the river. If anybody's looking for work, I got a job for you."

Squint Blear spit chewing tobacco. It landed in the dust and splashed her boots. "Afraid not, missy. Ain't much of a man who'd go to workin' for a woman — 'specially one in pants. A woman's made for better things. Where's yer husband? If he ain't around and yer lonely, I'm the one can fix you up proper, if you know what I mean." He sniggered, scratched his crotch, and turned away.

Suddenly he sailed into the street and landed on his belly. There was a footprint on his skinny butt. He pushed himself up, sputtering dust and tobacco juice. Hoots and jeers swooped around him like seagulls diving at tossed fish guts.

He stood and rubbed dirt from his eyes. "You shouldn't of done that, missy. Nobody, man or woman, gets away with kickin' Squint Blear in his sittin' down parts." He started toward her.

She turned and walked toward Seafoot's.

"Hey! Don't turn your back on me, bitch." He came at her fast from behind.

There was a loud click from the second wagon. Squint stopped quick and turned around slow. The cowboy had levered his rifle and was pointing it straight at Squint's crotch.

She didn't stop or turn around. "Thanks, Tom. If he moves one inch, shoot it off." She went into the store.

꿩 ꜩ

Seafoot threw the last bag of flour into the wagon and brushed down his dirty smock. He grinned, showing gold teeth. "That's all, Missy Hale. Ready to go now. Be careful by river, Missy. Crazy man there . . . live in bush. Have only one arm. Police say he kill somebody. They look for him but no catch. Be careful, hokay?"

"Thanks, Seafoot. I'll be careful. Besides, Tom is good with that rifle. If we see anybody, we'll let the police know." She got into the wagon and drove off.

They went south to the river. Tom slept in the willows near the water. She camped in a lean-to while they built a cabin. It was finished by first snow.

That night the wind moaned in the trees and sent branches crashing to the cabin roof. She lit a fire and the blaze printed shadows on the walls. The shadows joined and locked together, brutal and intense. The coupling was frenzied, no gentle dance.

Tom wanted her but she could not belong to him. He understood no other pattern between man and woman, so he stumbled through the snow and left the valley.

That winter, she lived by trap line and by fish caught under the ice. The following summer she had a baby, helped by a Cree woman who stayed a few days and fed the horses. The baby was fat and laughed a lot. She named him Tommy.

She raised horses, beautiful creatures. They roamed the valley while she made a ranch. To break them, she hired a half-breed who'd fought at Batoche. His name was Louis Garnot. He was wild as the buffalo he'd once hunted. She sold the horses he gentled. He stayed a season and then moved back to the prairie. She had a baby girl she named Louise, a sister for Tommy.

The town policeman was Andrew Sharpe. He used the pretext of searching for the one-armed crazy man to call on

Fay McHale. She sent him away, but he was smitten and kept returning.

Other men came calling. They were simple and direct in their desire but she refused them. Then she was pregnant again.

No one spoke it but the strain was real. The town held its breath. Each woman tried to recall her man's activities. Plans were made in case the baby should inherit a husband's name. The men denied all and thanked God she'd turned them down.

When the baby was born, she named him Andy. Mrs. Sharpe left to visit eastern relatives. She never came back. A short time later Andrew Sharpe turned in his badge and he, too, moved away.

Some of the women came to visit. They were curious and anxious, and they wished to see their worries up close. Fay McHale didn't welcome them. She was polite but made no friends. Unease crept around the town. It gnawed at the edge of people's comfort: Brandy Ross picked an argument with her husband at breakfast; Joy Austin shuddered when her husband left for work; Mary Adams made visits to her man's whiskey cache. Gradually unease turned to fear. The fear was malignant and spread through the town.

Down on the river bottom, Fay McHale raised horses and mothered her children. She was a demon for work and the ranch prospered.

Her nearest neighbours were the Blear family. They lived in a shack on Dogbone Creek, back from the river. Squint distilled home brew. He sold it to Seafoot on credit. He used the credit to buy groceries and short, grunting tussles with Seafoot's wife.

Tic Blear was Squint's woman. She talked a lot with Jesus. If Jesus wasn't around, she read the Bible out loud and tried again later. Ten years earlier Tic had produced twins, a girl and a boy, Toddles and Blinker. Every day for ten years Tic told them why God had sent them into the world.

"You're my punishment," she said. "God sent you here to give me a taste of hell. It's because I gave in to your pa's lust. I forgot about the Lord and rutted like the Whore of Babylon. Now I got you two, to remind me for the rest of my life. If I got to burn in hell, that's where you'll be too. You both come from sin and you both got the devil inside."

When Tic wasn't reading her Bible, she liked to think about the Reverend Carl Samson. She was a member of Reverend Carl's church. On Sundays she liked to watch him get wound up on heaven above, hell below and the sin between. When he stood in the pulpit, shouting for God and shaking his fist at the devil, she felt a flood of Christian love well through her body. She closed her eyes and imagined herself and Reverend Carl driving heathens from the vast prairie. The heathens were always Indian or Chinese.

Sometimes, early in the morning, she'd luxuriate in the haze between awake and asleep. Secure beneath her buffalo robe, she'd picture Reverend Carl with no clothes. He was handsome, dark and muscular. He'd pick her up in strong arms and carry her safe toward the sunset. They were alone. No heathens were left in the land. She would hear a gold trumpet. Reverend Carl would lay her down on the wide, pure prairie and lean over her. Then she'd force herself awake and scurry out of bed. She never allowed her fantasy free rein. She was afraid it might overwhelm her and she wouldn't be able to stop. After thinking about Reverend Carl, Tic had a terrifying energy. She used it to help save souls.

She decided to make Fay McHale her project. Tic liked projects. Her heart fluttered with bursts of charitable passion when she had a project.

"There's carnal and unchristian things happening out at the McHale place," she told Reverend Carl. "Babies are born out of wedlock. That woman has corrupted half the men in town. It's not good for kids to be around that stuff. They could grow up twisted. We should do something about it."

Reverend Carl had seen Fay McHale. He agreed she might be in need of a little guidance.

Early one Saturday he hitched a buggy to his horse, Delilah, and drove to the river. As he came into the McHale yard he saw someone on horseback head into the willows.

"Damn, I've missed somebody," he said out loud. The horse stopped at the sound of his voice. *I've got to quit using that word,* he thought. *It isn't right to be cursing when I'm doing the Lord's work.* He flicked the buggy whip and Delilah obligingly trotted a few steps.

He saw her standing under a cottonwood, drinking from a mug. The morning sun framed her mussed hair. She looked like she'd just got out of bed and thrown on clothes. He stared. Lord God, she was beautiful. He felt the resistance of fabric to flesh. Unconsciously, he brushed his hand over his trousers. The pressure was instant and intense. Desire clashed with duty. His soul was battleground and prize. The outcome would be sin or salvation. He squeezed his eyes and sent a silent plea to heaven. God heard and the pastor rose in him. Righteousness returned with fury.

Ah ha, he thought. *Someone's spent the night. I've caught the whore red-handed.* He grinned.

"Good morning, Mrs. McHale," he began. "I'm Reverend Carl Samson. I've come to invite you to services tomorrow morning."

She didn't answer.

Reverend Carl took her silence for guilt. "I see you've had company," he said. "Did I come at a bad time?" His face was bland, but smugness coated his words like honey covers toast.

She sipped her coffee and stared at him. "You must have seen Rose," she said. "She's a Cree woman who helps me with the children."

Liar, he thought. *That was a man rode into the willows or Delilah ain't no horse. I wonder who it was. No doubt he'll be staring at me in the pulpit tomorrow, innocent as a newborn rat.*

Aloud he said, "You been down here alone too long. Why don't you come to church? Bring the young ones. By the way, have they been baptised? I'd be prepared to do it, and when they're old enough, they can start Sunday school, even if they are bastards."

Reverend Carl didn't need to mince words. Only through him could her children be legitimate in the community. His was a terrible power; sometimes it overwhelmed him.

"I can probably get you some help down here too," he continued. "A woman alone needs help. There's lots of men in town with nothing to do except stand around and chew tobacco. I could find time to pitch in myself. How about it?"

She smiled. He felt a twinge, and again surged against his moral fabric.

"I know," she said. "I've met some of those men. But you see Reverend, I got all the help I need. The Indians are willing to work. Even better, they mind their own business — not like a lot of other folks around." She gazed straight at him.

"Yes, but what about your children? They need . . . "

"What do you think they need?" She cut him off and didn't let him answer. "They're doing fine. They got lots of love. They don't need high moral pronouncements."

Reverend Carl was persistent. "Yeah, but aren't you afraid out here alone? They've never caught that one-armed crazy man folks say lives along the river. There's places down here even Indians won't go. Don't you worry at nights?"

Of course you don't, he said to himself. *You got half the men in Tuckahoe coming here. You're probably safer at night than anybody in town.*

Fay McHale interrupted his reverie. "No thank you. Now, if you don't mind, I've got work to do." She drained her coffee, turned her back and headed to the cabin.

He reached for the buggy whip, then pulled his hand back. Who did she think she was? How dare she turn her back on him? She was nothing but a damn whore, and he a man of God. He jerked the reins. He heard her laughter as he whipped Delilah out of the yard in spurned fury.

Reverend Carl became obsessed with Mrs. McHale. Over the next few months he made the trip to the river many times. The crowd in front of Seafoot's began to think there was more to the visits than simple soul-saving.

Later that year she had another baby, a little girl she named Carla. Reverend Carl felt the hot steam of disgrace. Spurred by letters from his congregation, the church recalled him to a friendlier parish.

The message was clear. Fay McHale was not worth the risk. The men from town quit calling. No one wanted the disgrace. Without a word being spoken, Fay McHale became off-limits. For Tuckahoe's male population a trip to her ranch became as rare as a Sunday morning without a hangover.

Tic blamed Fay McHale for Carl Samson's disgrace. When she lay under her buffalo robe in the mornings, a picture of Reverend Carl, frolicking naked with Fay McHale, intruded on her fantasy. She tried to dismiss the image but it always returned. Worse, she found herself aroused, twice to the point of no return. Each time she felt drained and guilty. Her hatred for Fay McHale grew and became a bitter thing.

Toddles and Blinker liked to spy on Fay McHale. They would sneak through the willows and watch. They were the first to know that Tom, the original cowboy, had returned.

"That cowboy's come back over to the whore's place," Blinker announced through mouthfuls of rabbit stew.

"Don't go saying that word, even if she is one," Tic told him.

Blinker and Toddles giggled and ran outside. Squint toyed with his stew and didn't say anything.

Squint had never forgiven Fay McHale for embarrassing him. He nursed a grudge deep inside. It bobbed around in a small reservoir of lust the way ice floats in water. With time, grudge and lust mixed together like it was natural. Squint liked the feeling. It made his wrestles with Seafoot's wife more intense.

Seafoot told him one day, "Mista Blear, You can't wrestle with Wifey no more. She scared. She say you don't wrestle like before. She say you rough — maybe hurt her. You gotta stop, Mista Blear. Wifey can't make money if she hurt."

Time passed. The mixture in Squint fermented and bubbled up. It tasted sour in his throat. He tried to get Tic interested, but he was no match for Jesus. Tic reserved her passion for her own redemption, the memory of Carl Samson and her hatred of Fay McHale. She told Toddles and Blinker, "I decided if your pa wants to rut around like a big boar hog, he can damn well sleep in the pig pen."

Hearing about the return of Tom snapped something in Squint. He ruminated on his embarrassment. The mixture in him boiled over.

One day he saw Tom, on horseback, climbing out of the valley. *He's left the bitch alone,* he thought. *Time to pay a visit. I'll teach her to mess with Squint Blear.* The acid brew ate away his last restraint. He grabbed his rifle and headed downriver. Squint formulated no plan. Inside him vengeance and lust rode separate horses, but he knew they belonged in the same corral.

It was coincidence that Toddles and Blinker were nestled in the willows spying when Squint walked into Fay McHale's yard. She saw him coming. "You kids all stay inside," she told Tommy. Then she came out and closed the door behind her.

Squint pointed his rifle. He didn't say hello. "You and me got an old score to settle, bitch."

She looked at the rifle and the craziness in Squint's eyes. She didn't think reason would work, but it was all she had. "Mister Blear, why don't you put that rifle down so we can talk?" she said.

"Time for talkin's over. Take off yer duds."

"My clothes! Why are you doing this? Where's your wife?"

"Never mind the questions. Just get 'em off. I mean it."

She sighed and saw she had no choice. Her blonde hair was down below her shoulders. It framed high cheekbones and pale eyes. Her fingers freed the buttons on her shirt, starting at the top, down past her hard breasts. She let it slide off her shoulders.

Squint swallowed hard. Toddles and Blinker scrambled away to tell Tic.

Next, she pushed her trousers along her hips. They fell and she stepped from them. The sight of Fay McHale in underwear pulled Squint forward. He forgot everything. Lechery overwhelmed him. He was propelled toward relief the way lungs seek air. He dropped the rifle and tore open his shirt. He hopped on one foot, pushed off his pants and clawed at his long johns. His balance gave way and he fell in the dirt. Fay McHale stepped nimbly around him and picked up the rifle.

Squint lay in the dirt, his red long johns around his knees, tobacco juice on his chin. He was beyond thinking. His eyes were closed. When he opened them he was staring up the unwavering barrel of his own rifle.

Her eyes bored into his. "Get up and get your pants on, you son-of-a-bitch. You're going to meet the devil and it's going to be formal."

Squint's eyes were wide. More tobacco juice flowed into his whiskers. He was confused. It's hard to go from arousal to terror. Squint made the trip so fast, his brain didn't keep up. He lay in the dirt, mouth opening and closing like a fish in a boat. He couldn't understand. It's hard to look at your own death clearly, and Squint saw he was going to die!

Suddenly a shot drove birds from the willows. Squint screamed. Fay McHale looked up. She hadn't pulled the trigger.

Tic came out of the shadows holding a shotgun. It was pointed at Fay McHale. She was snarling. Her face was the colour of broken grapes. The snarls turned to screams:

"You weren't satisfied, whoring for half the country. You had to take my man too. When he said no, you forced him with a rifle. You're a bitch in heat. In your underwear in broad daylight. It's a good thing I got here in time, before you ruined him forever. I'm going to shoot you. The world will be better off."

Fay McHale dropped her rifle. On the ground, Squint howled and held his backside. The buckshot was painful.

❧ ❧

Tom was talking quietly to Jim Ackerman, the new policeman, when Toddles and Blinker galloped into town. They pulled to a stop in front of Seafoot's. "Our ma's gone to shoot our pa dead 'cause he's ruttin' with that whore downriver," Toddles shouted. "I think she's gonna shoot the whore, too. We was scared, so we took pa's horse and come to tell you, and . . . " Her eyes got wide. "The whore's almost naked!"

Ackerman didn't put much stock in kid's tales and was inclined to chase them away. However, on the chance that Toddles might be right about Fay McHale being naked, he decided to have a look.

He and Tom rode out of town, followed by the twins rocking on the back of Squint's giant nag. The crowd in front of Seafoot's had heard. Many decided to tag along. Others joined. Soon most of the town was heading to the river to watch Tic shoot Squint and the whore. It was a fine day and they joked along the way. Dogs followed the crowd.

They came through the willows into Fay McHale's yard. She was still standing in her underwear. Squint was squirming on the ground, holding his backside and moaning. The shotgun waved from Squint to Fay McHale and back again. Tic's eyes were clouded. She was uncertain what to do next. She hadn't let anyone move for over an hour.

The crowd saw what it had come for and lost its purpose. Some people milled around and made disapproving noises. Others simply watched. No one knew what to do next. There was no will in the gathering, just a hint of titillation wrapped in vague expectations. The murmurs gradually stopped. Only time and the shotgun moved. Everything else was still.

Jim Ackerman felt he should do something. Trouble was he didn't know what. *Might as well enjoy the show*, he mused. *Don't look like much of anything is going to happen.*

The cabin door opened and the McHale children came out. The oldest was carrying the baby, who was crying. They crossed the yard and stood by their mother.

The dogs started barking when they heard the baby. The noise drove the clouds from Tic's eyes. "See what I been telling you. The whore's naked and there's her bastards. They belong in hell. So do the men who been out here at nights, ruttin' and making these whelps. She's been sleeping with everybody. We should shoot her right now. Get rid of her once and for all." Tic's voice rose. "They're all bastards," she shouted. "They're the devil's runts."

Tom slowly raised his rifle. Ackerman put his hand out and touched Tom's arm. "Don't shoot her," he said. "If that shotgun goes off, it'll hit the kids for sure."

Fay McHale took advantage of the conversation to put on her shirt. Squint continued to moan. He pulled himself to his knees.

A man in the crowd shouted, "Don't put your clothes on, whore. We want to see what you are. Leave it in the open so there's no doubt." A few of the men laughed.

"Let's run her off," a woman's voice yelled.

"Yeah, take her and her horses and her bastard children and head 'em to the prairie . . . so far they never come back," someone replied.

The crowd quietened again and digested the idea. Many moved back to willow shade. The sun was higher. Some folks wished they'd brought something to drink. A few men produced whiskey flasks and passed them to friends. It was fine entertainment, better than the fall fair. Too bad it was so hot.

The dogs ran to the far side of the yard and barked into the willows. A tall man stepped out of the leafy shadows. He had a rifle. He pointed it into the air and fired. Tic shuddered and pulled her shotgun around to face him.

He walked toward her. The crowd gasped. He was unshaven and had long hair. His eyes blazed. He held the rifle in his right hand. His left arm was missing.

"It's the one-armed crazy man," someone shouted. "Get back before he kills somebody."

Everyone pushed farther into the willows. Hearts thumped. The crowd was no longer titillated. It was afraid.

Tic dropped her shotgun. She was a zealous woman but she too had heard of the one-armed crazy man. Her heart shivered.

Jim Ackerman's heart fell into his boots. He'd enjoyed the show as much as anybody, but now the danger was real. All eyes turned to him. He felt sick. Responsibility dropped on him like a hawk on a gopher. He forced his right foot past his left. His voice wavered. "Just a minute," he said. "I know who you are. Better tell these folks here. Don't do anything foolish, especially now."

The one-armed man stopped and stood by Fay McHale. He gazed at Ackerman. The dogs quit barking. No one moved. Tree leaves were limp in the heat. Folks stared at the space between events. The gap was troublesome.

Finally the man spoke. "I'm Robert McHale," he said. "This here's my family. Over there's my brother, Tom. What are you all doing here? You're standing on my land."

The crowd moved out from the willows. Everyone talked at the same time.

"But these can't be your kids."

"She's been sleeping with everybody in town."

"And she's been rubbing folk's nose in it by naming the bastards after the fathers."

"That first one's named after Tom, over there. He can't be your brother."

Robert McHale grinned. "Oh, they're my kids all right," he said. "And Tom is my brother. We figured naming the children like we did was a good way to get nosy folks, and men with other things on their mind, to stay away from a woman living alone. It worked too. Eventually I was able to spend most nights in my own home although I had to lay low during the day."

"Yeah, I can see why. You're the one-armed crazy man they say killed somebody." The crowd tensed. Somebody had drunk too much whiskey.

"I can answer that," Ackerman said. "That's what Tom came to tell me. McHale here's been wanted for killing a man over by Moose Jaw. Only he never done it. Someone else has owned up. He's been hiding down here for over four years. He was here even before his missus showed up. Tom showed me papers. McHale's in the clear now. You should all head home."

The crowd moved slow, reluctant. It had been a good show. Life can be tame after a good show.

In summer, heat shimmers to the edge of the prairie. You can see through the dancing air, but it distorts so things aren't always what they seem.

The TUCKAHOE WIND BREAKER

The road outside town rambles around dust dunes and strays by dried sloughs, wandering across the landscape like some folks meander through time; a politician's afterthought, it has no purpose and no destination. The town itself has no ambition. It slumps at the edge of the prairie, shiftless like a drifter on the side of the highway. The train still runs, but it too has lost its mission. It now arrives and departs without slowing down.

It wasn't always so. The railway was the anchor. Unbending, the track crossed the plain as if God had grasped both ends and pulled it taut. People built businesses and homes beside it. Farmers ploughed fields within listening distance of its lonely whistle. They clung to it and created Tuckahoe.

It was a time when folks went away on important trips to faraway cities, and the train brought in others with new plans and new ideas.

🙝 🙟

One hot August afternoon in 1903, it brought a tall, middle-aged man dressed in a dark suit and carrying a suitcase. He had the face of someone who knows better than to attempt to fill an inside straight, but retains enough optimism to try. The skin over his cheek bones wrinkled when he smiled. The smile itself ran along the bottom of his face as if the wrinkles were all his cheeks could manage and were too weak to pull up the ends of his lips. His black hair was parted on the right and combed meticulously to the left. Bushy eyebrows hung down and forced him to tilt his face up to see where he was going. This gave him an earnest, dignified look.

The man was Morton Goldsack, and after storing his suitcase with Mr. Dawson, the station agent, he strode onto Main Street, walking boldly in well-shined shoes like a banker on a mission of foreclosure. He moved with determination but sometimes hesitated, as if he had forgotten what he was determined about. When he reached Seafoot's store, he paused and stuck a thin cigar past a straggled moustache into one end of his horizontal smile. He fine-tuned the high collar on his white shirt and snugged the knot on a floral tie. Then he set his expression to the level of serious resolve and stepped through the door.

Morton toyed with the watch chain looped across his vest while his eyes adjusted to the light. He took in the counter with pipe and chewing tobacco displayed behind the glass. Tins of Malkin's Tea and Swift's Silverleaf Lard were stacked on shelves behind the counter. Razors, soap and repair items for ladies' faces rested on other shelves.

Bolts of fabric on the wall failed to muffle the disapproving voice of a short, skinny man dressed in a black suit. The voice was directed at an oriental lady perched on a stool behind the counter. "He'll burn in hell if he doesn't change his heathen ways," the man shouted.

His thin nose draped forward on his face like the crease on his trousers. A silver cross hung from a leather cord around his neck. He turned and shouldered Morton aside. "Out of my way, sinner," he said as he slammed through the door.

The oriental lady grinned and winked at Morton. She wore a man's shirt and a bowler hat that was pushed back to reveal wide brown eyes. "Hello Mista," she said. "I Miss An. That Reverend Harley Bentwhistle. He Methodist minister in Tuckahoe."

"What's his problem?" Morton asked.

"Mista Bentwhistle not like my husband, Seafoot." She waved toward a huge bald man who was dressed in a grey smock and playing click-clack on an abacus.

Seafoot flashed a gold-toothed smile and studied Morton with the straightforward look of someone who prides himself on his ability to size up strangers. Indeed, the success of his business depended on that ability. He had come from China to build the railroad but found he could make more money trading whiskey for beaver pelts, then pelts for supplies, then supplies for whiskey. He pocketed a piece of each transaction and eventually accumulated enough to buy the store. He sold groceries and dry goods in front and booze in the back. Outside, at the rear of the building, a covered stairway led to poker and other delights. He abandoned the abacus. "Welcome, Mista," he said. "You want supply, I got. You want drink, I got."

He watched Morton's response. Satisfied, he waved a heavily muscled arm toward the back of the store. Morton saw men standing in front of a bar that ran the length of the rear wall.

Seafoot continued, "You want poker, I got. You want wrestle with woman, I got . . . on Saturday."

A row of bottles stood along the bottom of a mirror behind the bar and on shelves beside it. They framed a reflection of everyone in the room. Instinctively, Morton flexed his dealing fingers. Then he put his hand in his pocket. *He was a newspaper man, not a gambler*, he reminded himself. The men at the bar were potential subscribers, not poker victims. He allowed a smile around the cigar. "Thank you, sir," he said to Seafoot. "I believe I'll have a whiskey."

He turned to the line of drinkers. "How do, gentlemen? My name's Morton Goldsack and I've come to Tuckahoe because it's been brought to my attention that folks here are sadly lacking in knowledge of local and national affairs. I aim to start a newspaper . . . you know, the fourth estate." He grinned and ran his fingers over his carefully combed hair.

Squint Blear, standing by himself at one end of the bar, turned, puckered, aimed, fired and scored a bull's eye in the nearest spittoon. He, his wife Tic and their unmarried daughter, Toddles, raised pigs down on Dogbone Creek. Squint was allergic to bathtubs, so he carried the evidence of his occupation wherever he went. The space around him could never be described as crowded. "You gotta be in the wrong town, Mister," he said. "We got no need for a newspaper. Folks here can spread scuttlebutt faster than the telegraph. Most of the local affairs is old news — lest of course, you're planning to have one yourself."

Morton looked him in the eye. "No, I don't plan to do that, but I am going to start a newspaper. Any of you folks read?" he asked. "I mean newspapers," he added.

Squint scratched his crotch and swiped at tobacco juice that had dribbled onto his whiskered chin. "Read?" he said. "Hell, half these boys never learned to talk proper, let alone read. You are in the wrong town, Mister."

One-armed Robert McHale raised horses downwind from the Blear place. He had a history with Squint, and as a matter of principal disagreed with everything his aromatic neighbour said. "Don't listen to him, Mister Goldsack," he said. "He's the only one around here can't read, unless you count recognizing the 'X' he uses for a signature."

Everyone at the bar laughed.

"You folks won't have to be ignorant anymore," Morton said. "I'll keep you informed. I'm a cultured scholar and a student of politics. During elections I'll tell you about the candidates and how to vote. I aim to print everything that happens and who does the happening. Nothing scares me."

Seafoot poured him a shot. "You make newspaper here, you need drink. Mista Bentwhistle and church folks not like newspaper."

"Thank you," Morton said and tossed back the drink. He grinned. "Not only that, boys, but I'm going to do it with no money, no partners, and no equipment. Now, about subscriptions . . . "

☜ ☞

He set up shop in a room above Seafoot's. His first one-page effort proudly bore the masthead, *The Tuckahoe Wind Breaker.* In the editorial, Morton explained the name:

"This paper will disseminate all breaking news faster than it could be carried by the wind."

He went on to declare himself a crusader, a champion of individual rights and lost causes, a man who never backed away from a fight. A note on the back of the page gave subscription details:

"This paper will be published weekly and will cost $4.00 per year. If the reader does not wish to be wearied by dependability, there will be a second paper published on a sporadic schedule. Its cost will be $1.00 per year. Unfortunately, subscriptions for the weekly paper are already sold out." (September 11, 1903)

Morton had a flair for sales and there was a ready response from merchants wanting advertising space. Seafoot took a half-page for the store. The paper grew to four pages.

The room he rented above the saloon was next to the one Miss An used to conduct Saturday night wrestling matches with some of the more sporting members of Tuckahoe's male population. She explained the arrangement to him. "Seafoot not real husband," she said, tossing her long black hair. "We say that so church ladies not get mad. I work in store and he let me use room." She lifted her chin and pushed it at Morton. Her eyes twinkled. "I business lady," she said.

A short, slender woman, her bubbly personality caused her high cheeks to crinkle when she was amused. On Saturdays she applied perfume liberally. The scent of lilacs masked the smell of men drinking themselves insensible in preparation for their day of rest. She dressed in a low-cut blouse, though her breasts were tiny. "Nothing there," she explained, "but blouse make men imagine. They see what they want to see. Horny man have bad eyesight."

"Why do you call it a wrestling match?" Morton asked. "And why only on Saturdays?"

"Ah," she said. "Wrestle is Seafoot's idea. He say people not like red-light place in Tuckahoe. Saturday is when men come to town. They want to do something so church is not waste of time on Sunday. I work in store on other days."

She flashed a quick smile and winked an oval eye. "I very good wrestler," she said. "I always win."

Morton looked at Seafoot working behind the bar. "Why do they call him Seafoot?" he asked. "Doesn't he have another name?"

"He not say other name," she said and laughed. "When he come from China, his English bad. First time on a ship, can't walk so good, fall down. Sailors say he need sea legs. Later, he make mistake and say he has no sea foot to walk on ship. It is big joke. Now, everybody call him Seafoot."

"Just one more question," Morton said. "How did you and Seafoot meet?"

"Ah," said Miss An. "He help me. One time, in Vancouver, a man hit me. Seafoot see and scare him away with meat cleaver. I stay with him. He my family."

Miss An's business was thriving. Men waited for Saturdays to test their mettle against the fearsome lady. During the week she wore a man's shirt and pants. When she tucked her long hair up inside a bowler hat, she resembled a teenage boy. "When I dress like boy, everybody understand, no wrestling match," she told Morton.

She didn't drink alcohol, but often joined her customers at the bar. Seafoot made tea for her. She was scrupulously honest and many of her customers gave her their money lest they get drunk and lose it. She usually ended up managing their finances, doling out allowances on Saturday night. "I am like bank," she said. "I keep money, then give back for man to spend in store, in bar or for wrestle."

Producing a sporadic paper was a sporadic occupation, so Morton frequently suffered from a scarcity of money and a surplus of time. Business was slow in the store during the week when farmers and cowboys were working, so he often passed the hours talking with Miss An and Seafoot.

"Normally, I make my living gambling," he said. "But it caught up with me. Most of the constabulary in the large towns know me, and I'm *persona non grata*."

"Why your person not grampa?" Miss An asked. "You not make babies when you young?"

Morton laughed. "I made my share," he said. "*Persona non grata* means I'm not welcome. Nobody wants me around."

"Ah, so nobody like you," Seafoot said.

"Right, Seafoot. Folks don't take kindly to losing money. In the last town, I left just ahead of the tar and feathers. Tuckahoe is the end of the line for me. I need to lay low for awhile."

"Why you start newspaper?" Miss An inquired.

"I made a bet with the owner of the *Stoneboat Creek Bugle*," Morton answered. "I won but the man had no money. The only thing I got was his damn printing press. The thing was too big to move so I made a deal with him. I let him keep the press in return for him printing the newspaper I aimed to start. All I do is put written copy in the mail and the papers come back on the train in a few days. About the time we shook on the deal, the police chased me out of town. All I got to show for my effort is the promise to print. Come to think of it, that's all I've got to show for a lifetime. So, to eat, I had to start a newspaper. My future as a gambler is all used up."

Seafoot poured a drink. "Here's to newspaper," he said.

🍃 🍃

One Sunday morning in early fall, Morton was carrying three freshly-shot mallards down Main Street when he recognized the Reverend Harley Bentwhistle and an opportunity he couldn't pass up.

"Good morning, Reverend," he said. "How's the soul-saving business?"

Reverend Bentwhistle stopped and tilted his head so he could stare up at Morton and down his nose at the same time. He had a sermon in his eyes that said "No nonsense!" to sin and sinners. "Oh, it's you, Goldsack," he sniffed.

"I been meaning to call on you, Reverend," Morton said. "I trust your collection plate is full these days. If it isn't . . . "

Reverend Bentwhistle cut him off. "I want to talk to you, Goldsack. You associate with the heathens that own the saloon."

" . . . perhaps you might try advertising in the *Wind Breaker*," Morton continued. "We have a discount for clergy."

"I should say not. I've read your stand on political and moral issues. We don't see eye-to-eye on anything. I will never advertise in your paper."

"That's your choice," Morton said. He moved to step around Reverend Bentwhistle and then stopped. "Could I at least sell you a subscription so you can keep up to date on what you don't like? You might find material for your sermons."

"Absolutely not!" Reverend Bentwhistle took his silver cross between his thumb and forefinger and brandished it as though fending off the devil. "I've got all the material I need in front of me. You've been hunting on the Sabbath. That's a sin in the eyes of God and the church."

"A sin, eh? Which commandment says I can't hunt on Sunday? You should make a list of all your so-called sins, Bentwhistle. I'll gladly print them. Folks should know when they're annoying you and your church."

The minister leaned forward and waved the silver cross. "I'm warning you, Goldsack. If you don't change, your soul will be damned for eternity."

Morton pushed the cross aside and strode down the street, mallard heads swinging on limp necks and hitting his leg with every stride. He went straight to his room and wrote an editorial:

"Why have Tuckahoe citizens allowed the clergy to take away our freedom on our one day of rest each week? It's time folks celebrated the Lord's Day as they see fit. If someone wants to play baseball on Sunday, it's his right to do so. If someone else wants to enjoy a drink or hunt ducks, rather than sit in a stuffy church listening to a fool, then that is also his or her right. This is no idle statement. I myself work on the Sabbath. I penned this message last Sunday while I sipped a beverage of the alcoholic variety." (October 9, 1903)

Reverend Bentwhistle read the editorial at breakfast. "Enough is enough. It's time for war," he told Mrs. Bentwhistle.

He went into his study and closed the door. For two days Mrs. Bentwhistle left his meals on the floor outside the study. She knew better than to disturb him when he was girding himself for battle. He emerged on the second day and waved a handful of papers under his wife's nose. His eyes blazed and wild hair waved above his unshaven face. "I've got it here," he shouted. "I'm going to broadside the *Wind Breaker* and that saloon at the same time. We're going to chase those sinners right off the prairie."

The town expected a response, and he faced a full house on Sunday morning. "There's evidence that a local establishment is a hotbed of iniquity, a devil's playground," he began. "There are rumours of carnal doings, lewd behaviour, drunkenness and gambling. If Moses had dealt with this house of Satan he would have needed fifty commandments. This place is not run by Christians. It's owned by foreigners. Only the Lord knows what pagan rituals they practice and they're certainly not married in the eyes of God. They're flourishing because of that newspaper. They couldn't advertise before it came to town. The editor had the nerve to ask me to promote my Sunday service in his rag. I told him, 'never,' and you should too. The paper and that saloon must close down, and the individuals that run them must leave our Christian town."

When Morton heard about the sermon, he didn't take it seriously. That was a mistake. Other churches sensed the *Wind*

Breaker was a threat to their standing in the community and joined Reverend Bentwhistle's campaign. Weekly they railed against Morton, Seafoot and Miss An. Pressure was applied to parishioners. Outlets for the paper dried up. Subscriptions were not renewed. Advertisers withdrew. People passed Seafoot's door and bought supplies elsewhere. Even Miss An noticed a drop in business. The situation became annoying, then serious, then critical.

"What we do?" Seafoot asked Morton. "I going broke."

"We need an issue," Morton said. "Something that will fire people up."

But no issue appeared. Time passed and Morton prepared for the worst. "I need to shut down soon," he told Miss An and Seafoot. "I have no money left."

"Me too," Seafoot said. "Maybe better in new town."

Seafoot adjusted a side of beef on his chopping block and aimed a meat cleaver.

"Maybe Seafoot and me should get married," Miss An said. "Then Mista Bentwhistle like Seafoot."

The cleaver sliced through the meat and buried itself in the chopping block. "Yee . . . ow," Seafoot yelled. "I cut damn finger. You crazy woman."

She laughed. "Is only joke. We friends. Marriage make friendship rotten like eggs in the sun." She picked a rag from the bar. "No worry," she said and wound the rag around Seafoot's finger.

"What did you mean when you said Bentwhistle would like Seafoot? What about *you*?" Morton asked.

"Oh, Mista Bentwhistle like me already," she said, and winked.

❧ ❧

The *Wind Breaker* had a "Question and Answer" column in which readers could request information and answers to queries. Most of the letters wanted recipes or answers to practical problems, such as sure-fire ways to rid a farm house of mice or how to kill warble larvae in a steer's back. One Monday morning a letter arrived requesting advice. Morton scratched his head. Then he read it to Miss An and Seafoot.

"What's the answer?" he asked. "I have no experience with this kind of thing."

The next issue of the paper carried the letter and a reply:

"DEAR EDITOR: i have never rote a letter before but i don't know wat else to do. i work for a big rancher in these neck of the woods. he works me hard and pays me littel. after i buy tobaco and shaving sop my wages is used up. my problum is my bosses dotter Miss Louise. She is bewtifull like a flowr. i luv her but cant say becuz i have no fewtur becuz i cant save any money to get a head. also ther is a low-down skunk in the pictur. his name is Peter Mellowfish Fundytooth [Ed. note: names have been changed to protect the reputations of individuals and low-down skunks]. he is one of them inglish remmitter men. He has lots of mony and my boss promised him he can mary Miss Louise. she dont know he is a low-down skunk who wants her dadies ranch and her bawdy for his own pleshur. she dont know im alive. wat shood i do? A HARD WORKING COWBOY.

ANSWER: The editor of this newspaper has little experience with this sort of problem, never having been ignored by the fair sex. Therefore, he has contacted a lady who is well-versed in matters of the heart. Her advice (edited for clarity) follows:

DEAR HWC: Yours is an age-old problem. I have two suggestions. First, ask your boss for a raise. He will be certain to respond favourably if you congratulate him on his athletic ability. Ask if his wife is aware of his skill at breaking wrestling holds, particularly the dreaded Chinese Double Thigh Lock. Ask your friends who it is that keeps their savings, and give your extra wages to that person to hold for your future. Second, you must deal with Mr. Fundytooth. He is in this country because no one wants him in England. These people are aptly described as pompous. Tell him he is not wanted here either. If he refuses to leave, I suggest you shoot him. Good luck, MRS. ANNIE C. FOOTE. P.S. Try growing a beard." (January 15, 1904)

Curiosity stampeded through town the way cattle run when they smell a bear. There was little doubt in anyone's mind as to the identity of the individuals in the letter. Trouble was, everyone's little doubt was different. The next issue of the *Wind Breaker* carried two more letters which provoked a modest increase in circulation and a larger increase in speculation:

"DEAR EDITOR: I am the individual referred to as Fundytooth in your last issue. I have never read a more belligerent diatribe and I take extreme umbrage at being called pompous. Let me state that I am proud of my English heritage as well as my ability to spell. I will not insult Louise by mentioning the nature of our relationship. Suffice it to say, she is far from the blushing flower of maidenhood your correspondent imagines. HWC was right in one respect. Louise's father has promised her to me. As my stipend from home will not last forever, it is imperative that we marry so I can take over her father's ranch. Be assured that when I do, HWC will be fired on the spot. I don't want to marry too quickly, though. There are many wild flowers on the prairie. Please desist in printing more badly spelled missives from that disgruntled manure pusher. Yours truly, PETER MELLOWFISH FUNDYTOOTH"

And:

"DEAR EDITOR: Please help me. Since I read his letter I have been waiting for HWC to declare himself. To date, he has not done so and I don't know who he is. I'm afraid I've committed a terrible indiscretion with Mr. Fundytooth and HWC will not be interested in me if he finds out I'm a wilted flower. We have been engaging in sin for three months. I was swept off my feet by charm, promises, and money. I don't love him but feel I must marry him because of my indiscretion. He said he would marry me but now says he can't afford it. I don't understand as he gets money from England and wins a lot more at poker. Is my situation hopeless? Respectfully, A WILTED FLOWER.

ANSWER: While your situation does seem hopeless, let me assure you there is always one more pickle in the barrel, although your choice seems to be between two pickles. Let's deal with the biggest one. You say Fundytooth has money, yet can't afford to marry you. Perhaps he doesn't have as much as he lets on. If he is good at poker, he should quit playing penny-ante with cowboys and engage in games where he can substantially increase his wealth. The writer knows of a game where Fundytooth will be able to buy England if he wins. Please advise him to contact me. EDITOR" (February 5, 1904)

Interest blazed up. Subscription requests came from as far away as Moose Jaw. Advice poured in for Hard Working Cowboy and Wilted Flower. Some folks wrote with suggestions for Fundytooth. Most of these were unprintable. Advertisers reappeared. More pages were added to the paper. At Seafoot's store, bets were taken on the as-yet-unscheduled poker game. Miss An held the money. The Question and Answer column in the next *Wind Breaker* was read by all:

"DEAR EDITOR: Fundytooth here. I am very interested in the poker game mentioned. Please advise. PMF

ANSWER: A game has been arranged through the auspices of this newspaper. EDITOR.

DEAR EDITOR: i want to thank Mrs. Foote for her advise. i asked my boss for a rase and he gave me a good one wen i menshun the Chinees Duble Thy Lok. i am saving my exter wages with a kind lady. Yor first advise was good so i hav decided to take your other advise. im goin to shoot Fundytooth. HWC.

ANSWER: Don't be in a hurry. Perhaps, when Mr. Fundytooth wins a lot of money, he will leave of his own accord. EDITOR.

DEAR EDITOR: I am aghast at your Question and Answer section. Shootings and immoral behaviour have no place in a newspaper. The young woman mentioned should go down on her knees and ask God's forgiveness for her sins. So should you, for publishing such a story. Repent now. REVEREND HARLEY BENTWHISTLE.

ANSWER: Thank you for your letter and for your interest in my newspaper. It's good to know the clergy have blessed my small effort by reading the *Wind Breaker*. I am pleased to provide you with a free one-year subscription. Your patronage and that of the church is appreciated. EDITOR" (March 4, 1904)

Suddenly Morton was faced with a dilemma. Increased correspondence, requests for advertising and demand for the paper forced him to print on a regular schedule. He found himself rising an hour before the town's roosters. For the first time in his life he had a regular job. Seafoot's store was packed day and night with men hoping to witness the poker game. Miss An was run off her feet. She extended her wrestling hours to include Friday.

"It's getting to be too much," Morton told Seafoot. "I didn't bargain on working round the clock. Something has to give."

"Don't worry," Seafoot said. "Make money now. Rest later."

But Morton was tired. He suspended publication of the *Wind Breaker* for two weeks and went fishing. Reverend Bentwhistle claimed victory. "We did it," he chortled to his congregation. "We closed the blasphemer down."

His chortle was premature. Morton returned with a mess of jackfish and a mass of energy. On the following Saturday, a single page issue of the *Wind Breaker* was delivered free to every house in town. It contained one letter and an answer:

"DEAR EDITOR: I want you to know that HWC and I are together and very much in love. Fundytooth has left town. HWC thinks he was afraid of being shot but I think it's because he lost all his money in a poker game. HWC told me the lady that keeps his savings bet on the game and made a lot of money for him. So he has asked me to marry him. We are both happy. Thank you. A FORMER WILTED FLOWER

ANSWER: The editor of this newspaper extends best wishes to HWC and FWF. All's well that ends well. He also urges the happy couple to take their wedding vows as soon as possible. Surely, Reverend Harley Bentwhistle would be pleased to tie the knot and provide guidance, so the happy couple can start their married life unencumbered by prior events. He is eminently qualified to advise others as he is a veteran of the war against lubricity. Armed only with a silver cross, he has, on many occasions, climbed the stairway to lechery and faced down lewdness in its lair. At times, these encounters were so intense that the good Reverend lost parts of his attire, but he never lost his rigid motive force. This editor was privileged to witness one of these contests recently, and he came away with new respect for the potency of the good man's onslaught. The term "straight and narrow" does not do him justice. Our man of God prevailed with weapon intact, although he lost his silver cross. Fortunately, this editor was able to retrieve it. He may claim it at any time. EDITOR" (April 15, 1904)

Morton was standing upwind of Squint Blear when Reverend Bentwhistle came running into Seafoot's. He wrinkled his nose as he passed Squint and looked around the room before stopping beside Morton at the bar. "Good afternoon, Mr. Goldsack," he whispered.

"Afternoon, Reverend," Morton said. "What can I do for you?"

"You have something that belongs to me, Mr. Goldsack. A silver cross. It was a present from my mother." He spoke into his chest and focused his eyes on the bottles behind the bar.

"Yes I do, Reverend. I have it in my pocket." Morton reached into his pocket and extracted a thin cigar. He made no further move.

"I . . . I'd like it back, Mr. Goldsack, please."

"Certainly, Reverend. There's just one thing." Morton lit the cigar and puffed up a cloud of smoke.

"Oh . . . oh, really . . . ah, you mean a reward. Certainly. What do you . . . "

Morton cut him off. "No, I don't want a reward, Bentwhistle. I was thinking about advertising." He exhaled and Reverend Bentwhistle stepped back.

"Of course, Mr. Goldsack. I was thinking about that myself. The church is prepared to take a half-page."

Morton took the cigar from his mouth. "I was thinking more along the lines of a full page, Reverend."

The minister looked Morton in the face for the first time. "You're right, Mr. Goldsack. We do need a full page. Consider it done. I trust there will be no further mention of this."

"Sure, Bentwhistle. We understand each other." Morton pulled the cross from his pocket and held it out.

Reverend Bentwhistle surveyed the room again. Then he snatched the cross from Morton's hand and slipped the cord over his head. "I have a question." he said. "The couple . . . from the letters. They haven't come in. Do you know why?"

"I sure do, Reverend. I had a note from them. They eloped. Left this part of the country to get away from all the attention."

Squint, down the bar, choked on his drink and spun around. "Damn it, I knew it. Those letters were from my daughter, Toddles. She made up the part about her daddy being rich. She ran off last week, though I didn't think she went with no cowboy. Well, spice my britches, I never thought we'd marry her off. Things is turning out okay."

Squint walked out of the store. Reverend Bentwhistle followed him through the door. Morton was left alone at the bar.

Seafoot poured him a drink. "Did you know girl in letter was Squint's daughter?" he asked.

Miss An giggled from behind the counter. "Girl not Squint's daughter," she said and laughed out loud. "There no girl, no remit man, no cowboy. Morton make it up. Is all pretend."

Seafoot looked puzzled for a moment, and then he too laughed. "What about cross?" he asked.

Miss An giggled again. "I take when Mista Bentwhistle come for wrestle," she said. "I give to Morton."

Morton smiled and downed his drink. "Sorry folks, I have to go to work," he said. "I've got a deadline to meet."

GORDON TAYLOR LIVINGSTONE

Almost everything about the prairie is different from the land beyond. The plants are different. The animals are different. Even the sky is different.

Some say the woods close down a man's soul. That's wrong. Living in the bush concentrates the soul so it knows only one thing, but that one thing is vital and lasts a lifetime. The prairie expands the soul. Under the wide sky there is no focus. Because of this there are no boundaries, hence no end to a man's vision.

The only intersection between trees and plains occurs in the human heart. It alone can transcend time and place and circumstance. It alone can fathom love.

People rarely learn to live in both places. Even the Cree differentiate themselves. They are known as *Saka Wiyiniwak* and *Paskwa Wiyiniwak*, Wood People and Prairie People. They visit, but each shies away from living where the other makes a home. Home is more than location. It's what you know and are comfortable with. To be truly at ease in a place, you must become part of it — as much as a wolf or pine tree is part of its surroundings.

Woods and plain allow no free ride. What you take from them must be repaid and repayment has many forms. The fortunate do it with hard work and reverence. Some part with their integrity and peace of mind. Still others give up sanity. A few die. Wealth sometimes allows a man to delay this reality.

Even with money, however, there are responsibilities to which some cannot adapt, and without adaptation there is only bleakness and an early end.

There are folks who live on the fringe, people who frequent both regions but know neither. They avoid their debt by moving to one place when overwhelmed by the other.

⁊ ☙

Gordon Taylor Livingstone was such a man. He started life in England and he ended in the shadows between two worlds, a remittance man who had lost his remittance. Bad judgment had forced him from the culture he knew to the never-land between woods and plain, a land into which he'd not been born and which was as alien to him as a catechism to a trapper's whore. A gentle man of letters, the roughness horrified him, and the easy cruelty to man and beast made his stomach roll.

Gordon gave the impression of not being where he was standing so people rarely saw him. In the fall no one noticed when he grew his winter beard. In the spring no one noticed when he shaved it off. Folks lost the memory of Gordon's arrival and he supplied no past. To them he was a nondescript entity unencumbered by prior facts. He lived in the trees and ventured out only when driven by a craving, a craving generated by a lonely and appalling situation, a craving to speak and listen, a craving to understand and be understood.

Gordon Taylor Livingstone was a married man, but his family was no antidote to the terrible loneliness that ate through his well-being and gnawed at his sanity. He, his wife Marnie and their crazy daughter, Victoria, lived in a cabin amid the circumstances Gordon constructed.

Step by critical step, in the manner of a politician working toward election, Gordon built a life in this outlandish place.

But just as electoral fantasy leads to swollen expectations, Gordon's life became bloated by failure.

It's not fair to say he had a reputation. Reputation implies something outside the norm. Gordon's norm was failure. The only facets of his life that didn't end in miscarriage were those he aborted.

He never completely disconnected from his past. He kept one treasure, a medal depicting Queen Victoria at her coronation. A gift from his mother, it was his touchstone to faded memories . . . memories of youth, of a social life, of family, of university and lively discussions. It symbolised all he once had and could never have again. It rarely left the cord around his neck.

He had not learned proper ways to hunt, trap, fish or grow things. He survived by raising a few cows, a few goats, some chickens and a garden he scratched out in a new location each year. Long ago he'd decided there was no point in striving in this world. It was enough to keep the three of them existing.

Gordon had one source of income. In order to get cash to buy staples and other necessities, he had learned the arts of fermentation and distillation. When he felt the urge for company he hitched up his skinny nag, Shakespeare, and, riding in regal splendour on a stump in the middle of a stoneboat he took jars of his product to folks who lived near enough to be called neighbours. He never indulged in his own merchandise. His tastes were too refined for that. Only store whiskey passed his lips, and only to excess on appropriate occasions. Between these episodes he lived in an uneasy three-way compromise, balanced precariously between nature, his own needs and those of his family.

He loved them but his was not an easy family to love. His wife, Marnie, was a bird of a person, deficient in size and intellect. She did not speak or smile. Her only expression was alarm and she lived by it. Her nervousness knew no limits and bound her to the shadows. Conversation frightened her; she faded away at the sound of words.

No one knew from what swamp Marnie had been reclaimed. Some said he found her in the bush. Others thought he'd picked her from the street of a large city before he came to Tuckahoe. It was apparent she loved him for it. She devoted herself to his comfort. They never talked but she showed her feelings in a hundred ways. She had been wounded and he'd bound a splint to her spirit.

Marnie was a collector. She saved paper. Through the years she'd filled the cabin with it. She had boxes of ancient newspapers, piles of magazines, folded wrap from the general store, old letters and cartons of scrap. If paper production had been retroactive she could have treed the plains. She loved to fold it into different shapes and then spend hours feeling its texture and listening to the sound it made as she crumpled and ripped it; but the printing on the paper meant no more to her than a fly on the cabin wall.

Whenever Gordon was down, she cheered him by bringing out her latest treasure and let him listen as she tore it to shreds. He would marvel at her simplicity and pat her gently on the head. Then he would slip the Queen Victoria medal from his neck and let her hold it while he explained in slow detail the life they would one day have in England. "We'll live by the sea," he said, "and we'll travel to London in a fine carriage."

Marnie rubbed the medal against her cheek and her eyes shone as Gordon explained a landscape far beyond her understanding: meandering trout streams, lanes shaded by archways of green trees and distant hills that melted in vapoury sunlight.

Years before, they had collaborated in the creation of a child. At least it looked like a child. Like all of Gordon's constructions, this one was flawed. They named her Victoria after the long-dead Queen. As she grew it became apparent Victoria had inherited neither Gordon's capacity for speech nor her mother's predilection for silence. At first, she just whimpered and moaned. Later, she learned to scream, piercing shrieks that flew from the bush to blend with the howls of coyotes, screams that darted past shabby farms to reverberate in the cluster of shacks called Tuckahoe.

Gordon and his family stayed in the bush, away from the scrutiny that comes with open prairie. In winter they confined Victoria to the cabin. In summer they tethered her on a leash in the yard. Occasionally she slipped her harness and went trundling out from the leafy safety into the glare of the wide plain. A neighbour would go for Gordon. He'd bring the leash, gently soothe her and slowly lead her home.

Victoria was large. Despite a vacancy, she was unable to dwell in her head. Thoughts did not develop from the emotions that swirled behind her clouded eyes. She could not share Marnie's love of paper or Gordon's love of the writing on it. In the absence of intellect her life became eating and she grew huge. Her size limited her range, so Marnie often released her on their daily trek to the edge of the bush. She waddled along the horizon backed by the wide, dark sky that creeps to the tree line. A locomotive of a thing, she'd pick her way to open land and snuffle there, where once buffalo had wallowed. Always she was presided over by a watchful Marnie.

If you approached Gordon and Marnie's cabin with surprise in your step, all two hundred and fifty pounds of Victoria would be sitting in the yard, pegged to her leash, playing in the dirt, humming along while Marnie sang. The song wasn't real. The words didn't exist. Marnie made rhythm in her throat and Victoria mimicked the sound.

In January of Victoria's twentieth year, the wind drove snow from the plain and piled it to the tree tops. The temperature dropped so low it penetrated the logs in the cabin and they split with a crack like a hunter's rifle. The loud noise frightened Victoria. She screamed, but the sound had nowhere to go. A terrifying wail, it bounced from floor to rafter and skittered along the frozen wall. Scream piled on agonising scream, hour after agonising hour. Gordon identified the days of icy howls as an appropriate occasion for human and liquid company.

He harnessed Shakespeare and headed for Tuckahoe, stopping along the way to trade brew for money. Then he went to Seafoot's Saloon to buy real whiskey. He liked Seafoot's. The human debris at the bar revelled in Gordon's naiveté and ignorance. He, in turn, marvelled at *their* naiveté and ignorance. It was a fair trade. Each fed off the other, each made the other feel good and each had no idea what the other talked about.

"Good evening, gentlemen," Gordon said as he came through the door. No one looked up.

"Good evening," Gordon repeated, a little louder.

A few of the men standing at the bar glanced around and then turned back to their conversation. It was Saturday night and every inch along the bar was filled by men preparing hangovers as an excuse to skip church on Sunday morning.

"Excuse me, sir," Gordon called to Seafoot, who was pouring drinks. "I'd like a whiskey, please."

Seafoot didn't look up.

Gordon stood on his toes and waved his arms, trying to be seen. Seafoot continued to pour drinks. Gordon jumped and waved. He did it again. Then again. He glimpsed himself in the mirror behind the bar each time he jumped. The man in front of him turned around. "Cut it out, you goddam jackass-in-a-box," he said.

Seafoot looked up. "Whiskey, please," Gordon shouted.

"It's the crazy Limey," a cowboy down the bar said to the man in front of Gordon. They both laughed and turned back to stare at themselves in the mirror.

Seafoot poked a glass through the line of men. "Here, Mista Livingstone, you whiskey."

Gordon took the glass and began patrolling. He spotted a small opening and squeezed between two cowboys arguing how long it takes horseshit to freeze. "On a night like this, it's solid before it hits the ground," said the cowboy on Gordon's left. "That's why it bounces."

"Bullcrap," said the cowboy on Gordon's right. "Sparrows flock to it. It can't be froze."

"It's a bitter evening," Gordon ventured.

"Sure is," said the cowboy on Gordon's left.

"It must have been like this when Ymir, the first Frost Giant, was formed in icy chaos in Niflheim," Gordon said.

The cowboy stared at Gordon. "It's cold enough to freeze the knob off a marble stallion," he said.

"I guess Norse mythology isn't your forte," Gordon replied.

He stayed far into the night, talking, listening and exercising atrophied intellectual muscle. He left for home atop his stump, loudly singing "God Save the Queen". Then he dozed as the stoneboat glided over the icy trail. Shakespeare was well-trained and knew the way.

The horse stopped as they entered the yard. Something was wrong. The smell of smoke invaded Gordon's dream. He lurched awake. Fuelled by Marnie's paper, flames were shooting through the cabin roof.

Terror ripped into Gordon like a wolf rips into a fawn. It knocked the alcohol from his brain. His loves and his life were an inferno. He heard Victoria's scream as he kicked in the door. The smoke blinded him. He followed his ears and stumbled over her on the floor by the far wall. He pulled at her but she was panicked and refused to budge. Like a wounded beast, her wails echoed through the smoke. He found her hands. Gripping them, he dragged her, inch by inch, toward the door. Fire burned on the blanket wrapped around her. He went through the door, took a deep breath, and rolled her away from the cabin. Then he turned and went back to find Marnie. A second later the roof collapsed, sending sparks and flames high into the dark pines.

ೀ ೀ

Some animals survive by changing colour with the seasons, others by sleeping away a harsh winter, but for Marnie and Victoria there was no compromise with nature. They were found not far onto the prairie. Marnie was in front holding the leash. She had fallen. In her burned hand, she clutched a Queen Victoria coronation medal. Victoria, attached by her harness, was behind. She died sitting upright. They were hard to find. It had snowed after they froze. They blended perfectly with the landscape. They almost seemed a part of it.

The PIANO BOX

Some days, when folks are feeling low, they look at their town on the edge of the prairie and say it truly is the end of the world. They may be right, but it wasn't always that way. The ragamuffin boys, who used to climb the water tower beside the railroad track, could see it wasn't even close to the end of the world.

Going north, the trees — tamarack, spruce, birch and poplar — stretched for miles, and the escarpment rose to the sky as it made its way to the Arctic Circle. Hidden in the trees were lakes that had never been mapped. Flowing into the lakes were rivers that had never been fished.

It was a shadowy place. Indians and Métis moved through it. Farther back, where Indians didn't go, there were others — people who didn't exist. The government had no record of their births. No church had ever issued a baptism or marriage certificate. They were not on tax rolls. The property they lived on was not registered. They had never held a job or attended a public school.

They lived by trap line, fishing and hunting. Occasionally, after dark, one or two would slip into town to sell homebrew or Seneca root. They might buy tea or salt. They left quickly, before anyone got curious, but everyone knew they were there, even the police. It just seemed like too much trouble to go chasing back into the bush. Besides, they never bothered anybody. The Métis called them Les Ombres: the shadow people.

🕊 🕊

The town was Tuckahoe. It was a quiet place, like an under-taker's office or an empty outhouse, so folks felt a need for entertainment. They filled the need by meeting the train when it came from the west. Next day, they added more spice to their lives by welcoming the same train as it arrived from the east.

One spring evening the ragamuffin boys were watching from the water tower when the Seven O'clock Daily steamed into town. The welcoming committee was disappointed. No passengers got on or off. Only the freight was left sitting at the end of the platform for Sam Piper to deliver. There were lumber, dry goods, groceries for Seafoot's store — the things that kept commerce alive in a small town.

One thing was different. The boys left the water tower to see for themselves. Sitting in the freight pile, as out-of-place as a petticoat in a pulpit, was a huge piano box addressed to Mr. Lamar Quinlan. There was no return address. Folks couldn't figure it out. No one had heard of Lamar Quinlan. Sam was puzzled, too. He had no idea where to deliver the box. Besides, he didn't know anyone in town who could play a piano except for Aggie Parker, and she already had one.

He loaded the rest of the freight and left the box. Mr. Quinlan would show up eventually. One didn't order a new piano and then leave it sitting on a railway platform. There was no return address, so on the platform was where it was going to stay.

Later that evening when Mr. Dawson, the station agent, had gone to bed, and no one was around except for coyotes and hooty owls, the ragamuffin boys sneaked from their beds to see what was in the box. It was dark at the end of the platform. As they got close they heard the sound of wood breaking. They watched from the shadows as a hole appeared in the side of the box. It got bigger and a man emerged, dressed in a long coat and carrying a rifle. The boys crept deeper into the shadows.

The man was Lamar Quinlan of Harlan County, Kentucky. His face was the colour and texture of an old saddle. He had the hard look of a man who deals with disappointment by shooting at it. The boys sneaked back to their beds. Lamar Quinlan shouldered his rifle and stepped away from the shadows. He'd shipped himself to a new country and a new life.

In the morning he moved the piano box off the platform. He sat down inside it and stayed there for fifteen days, leaving only to shoot grouse outside of town. He cooked the grouse on a fire beside the platform. Mr. Dawson thought he might burn down the station.

"I want you to move off railway property," he told Lamar. "You got no business lighting a fire here."

Lamar stared at him, spit chewing tobacco, pulled his coat tight and sat down facing the fire. Mr. Dawson decided the danger wasn't that great after all.

For fifteen evenings Lamar stood by the tracks when the train pulled in. Then a woman arrived. She was skinny and pregnant, with the furtive look of someone who thinks the world is gaining on her. Lamar nodded. Harriet Quinlan hoisted her bag and followed him down the street. They left the fire burning by the platform.

Lamar hauled the piano box to the edge of town and it became their first home. They kept to themselves and spoke to no one. He went to work for Sam Piper and carted freight. Mrs. Quinlan fed herself and Lamar by picking berries and producing a garden beside the piano box. One day she also produced a baby girl they named Carrie-Ann.

Although the birth was difficult, it would later seem to both parents that Carrie-Ann arrived with a smile on her face. She came with a mane of black hair and wide, intelligent eyes that constantly took in the world around her and reflected back a sunny disposition. She was a silent child who demanded little and rarely cried.

In spring, when ice jams the river, a tremendous pressure is created. Backed-up water tries to break through to the empty space on the other side of the ice. When it does, it roars out of confinement until a balance is reached. Like the water, a town can't stand an empty space. Pressure builds and those charged with maintaining equilibrium rally to the purpose. So it was that representatives from the local Society to Promote Righteousness, Ethics and Etiquette arrived at the piano box with the expressed intent of asking Mrs. Quinlan to join them, and the unexpressed intent of filling the gap in their knowledge of the Quinlan's prior life.

Joy Austin knocked. Harriet Quinlan, holding Carrie-Ann, appeared at the hole in the side of the box. Her hair was pulled back in a knot. She had the resigned look of someone who has got caught running from the world. "Yeah," she said.

"Good afternoon, Mrs. Quinlan. My name is Joy Austin, and these ladies are Mrs. Adams and Mrs. Ross."

"Uh-huh," said Harriet.

"We're from SPREE and we've come to ask if you'd be interested in joining."

"What?" said Harriet.

"SPREE. We want you to join us," said Joy Austin.

"Oh," said Harriet.

There was silence. "Well?" asked Mary Adams.

"What?" said Harriet.

"Our SPREE," said Joy Austin. "Are you interested?"

"Don't drink," said Harriet. "No money."

"Oh, my goodness," said Mary Adams. "None of us drink . . . and membership is free. All you have to do is answer a few questions."

"What?" asked Harriet.

"Nothing much," said Mary Adams. "We just need to know where you used to live and why you came to Tuckahoe."

Another silence. "Oh," said Harriet.

"Well," said Joy Austin. "Where are you from?"

Carrie-Ann waved her tiny fists and grabbed her mother's hair. Harriet left the hole in the side of the box. She didn't come back. Joy Austin knocked again but the hole remained empty. "I guess she doesn't want to join," said Joy Austin.

The ladies turned and, speculating loudly, retraced their steps into Tuckahoe.

Harriet told Lamar about the visit. The next morning the Quinlans moved away. They went past cultivation, past the edge of the prairie, through the low bush, crossed swampland and climbed the escarpment. They left the Métis settlements and Indian camps behind.

They found the others, folks like themselves who had left the outside world to live in a place with no questions, folks whose lives the pine trees had swallowed, folks who lived in quiet dread of one day being coughed up.

They liked life in the bush, where the blend of high spruce, birch and poplar blocks sunlight, and the earth is a cool mixture of shadows and pine needles. Here, on the far side of a small lake, Lamar and Harriet built a cabin. Here they made a home and raised a family. Carrie-Ann was joined by four brothers and sisters. Lamar trapped, fished, and hunted. Harriet planted new gardens and picked more berries. Years passed. A new crop of ragamuffin boys hatched and grew in Tuckahoe.

Carrie-Ann became a slender, happy child who loved the silence beneath the miles of leafy green canopy that formed a ceiling in her backyard. She trailed behind Lamar and became proficient with traps and fish lures before she was ten years old. She never learned to speak and most of her thoughts remained behind her dark eyes, inaccessible to those who loved her. She played with her brothers and sisters but occasionally she would fade into the bush, returning hours later with a snared rabbit or a fish, gutted and scaled, ready for the fry pan.

Out there, away from righteous and pious influences, folks don't have the time or inclination to talk to God. So sometimes, in the midst of winter, God talks to them. The snow blows and drifts go to twenty feet. Even animals don't move. Trap lines get buried and the ice gets too thick to fish. Meat stored in the icehouse is used up. Berries canned in the fall get eaten. Hunger races through the trees. Then these folk who live in the shadows must look to the outside or face starvation.

🙰 🙰

Dick Muller lived between the two worlds. He had a florid face and the physique of a man whose only exercise was carrying his own ego. He never learned to read or write, but he could count money faster than a three-handed bank clerk. He traded with both sides and was one of the few outsiders familiar with Les Ombres. Dick would trade anything, but mostly he made his living with cattle. He didn't raise them, put them to pasture or butcher them. He bought and resold them. If conditions were right, he could buy them for half of what they were worth and sell them for triple what he'd paid.

At this crucial time, in the dead of winter, Dick got enjoyment out of life. While others sat next to their kitchen stoves and eyed the skies with trepidation, Dick squirmed with well-being. A flush of self-satisfaction drained from each whiskered jowl and settled with a gurgle in his ample paunch. He saddled his best horse and, singing to himself, he followed the ice trails. Eventually he found what he was looking for, a family so poor and hungry they were eating canned gopher and keeping their last dried-up cow alive in their cabin — people who needed staples so bad, they stank of malnutrition.

"How do," Dick beamed, tracking snow into the cabin. "I bet you're happy to see me. I've come with the milk of human kindness in my heart. I figure it's my God-given duty to help those less fortunate, and . . . " He surveyed the cracks in the walls and the sick baby crying in a box on the table. "If there's anybody less fortunate, you're it."

"We need medicine for the baby," the woman whispered from the shadows.

"And I need that animal tied in the corner. Looks like we can deal," Dick said.

He produced salt to put on the gopher and some gruel for the baby. Then he offered a minimum of cash and concluded the purchase. If someone was reluctant, Dick used persuasion. He simply said he was on good terms with the authorities and they were interested in who was here in the bush. This always brought recalcitrants around. He wasn't a greedy man. He did pay something for the animals. Sometimes, the milk in his heart barely curdled.

The following weekend, Sam Piper and a Métis kid were hired to take a large-box sleigh, pulled by Dick's magnificent team of grey Percherons, and make the rounds. They loaded beasts so starved they didn't resemble anything living. Then they paid the few promised dollars. Dick never went back on a deal.

The families had eyes as hungry as the animals they sold. "I hope he rots in hell," a husband muttered.

"Why don't you eat the damn cow?" Sam asked.

The answer was always the same. They needed blankets, or medicine for a sick baby, or a dozen other things to get through the winter. These were more necessary than one skin-and-bones cow that wouldn't produce a calf in the spring anyway.

🙡   🙟

Dick's wife had died years before. Some said she wasted away because of the orneriness of the man. He was the type you could talk to every day and still die of loneliness.

On one of his trips Dick spotted Carrie-Ann, who was now fourteen. She was a beautiful girl with flashing eyes and glistening black hair, wild and shy as a forest deer. Domestic chores were not for her. She preferred solitude, away from the cabin, away from the effort of trying to communicate without speech. She knew the back country better than most folks know the inside of an outhouse door and she could butcher a deer or skin a weasel slicker than bark peels from willow branches.

Dick decided she would be his new wife. He told Lamar and Harriet, "You folks don't exist back here, so there'd be no point churchin' this wedding. I'll just take her along when I go."

"Oh no!" gasped Harriet. Her face had the empty look of someone who no longer tries to keep ahead of the world.

"Uh-uh, Mr. Muller," Lamar said. "She's too young to leave home."

Dick's eyes removed Carrie-Ann's clothes. "Don't worry. I'll look after her good, Quinlan."

"Christ, Muller. She's only fourteen," Lamar said. "Find somebody your own age."

"Goddamn, Quinlan. Don't you understand? She's my wife, startin' tonight, or I'm talkin' to somebody down there where you come from."

Lamar had no choice. He had other young ones to feed. If Dick Muller turned him in, only the Lord knew how they'd survive.

Dick took Carrie-Ann back to his house. She did his cooking, she did his cleaning, she scrubbed the floors, she killed chickens and ironed shirts. When he was in the mood, he drank and spent the night taking away her childhood. He replaced it with degradation, and when he was finished, if he was sober enough, he beat her 'til she crawled.

By the time she was fifteen, Carrie-Ann had seen more of the dark side than most women would encounter in three lifetimes. Her eyes turned blank, but sometimes, when he slapped her hard, they glittered like a knife blade.

🖘 🖚

One day the ragamuffin boys saw Lamar driving a wagon with a piano box on the back. It was pulled by a magnificent team of grey Percherons. He went straight to the railway station and shipped the box on the evening train. Mr. Dawson said it was addressed to the sheriff in Harlan County, Kentucky.

Shortly after, someone noticed Dick wasn't around anymore. The girl was gone by the time folks went looking. Rumour was she went back to the bush.

Dick Muller was never found. The matter wasn't pursued much. Few folks had an interest in finding him. Mr. Dawson did send a wire to the sheriff in Harlan County. The reply he got didn't surprise anyone. It seems a large box had been delivered and left standing on a rail platform. Inside was a man's body butchered like a hunter's deer. It had been skinned slicker than peeled willows.

It had been impossible to say who it was, but papers in the box identified it as someone wanted for years in that neck of the woods, a man named Lamar Quinlan. They couldn't check it out, however: apparently there was no return address.

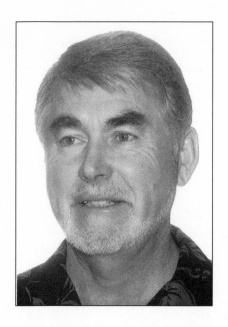

NEIL McKINNON is the winner of the 1999 CAA International Writing Contest and the 2004 El Ojo Del Lago Best Fiction Award (Mexico). His work has been published in Canada, Japan, Mexico, and the U.S. He has been a freelance writer for several high-profile Canadian newspapers such as the *Toronto Star* and the *Calgary Herald.* He lives in Canada and Mexico.